Main by Southwest

Celeste Harmer

Published by Celeste Harmer, 2024.

This is a work of fiction. Similarities to real people, places, or events are entirely coincidental.

MAIN BY SOUTHWEST

First edition. October 25, 2024.

Copyright © 2024 Celeste Harmer.

ISBN: 979-8227986153

Written by Celeste Harmer.

Also by Celeste Harmer

The World I Know: The Diary of a Southwest Philly Girl
Main by Southwest

Table of Contents

PART ONE 1
June 1983 2
Chapter One 3
Chapter Two 13
Chapter Three 19
Chapter Four 25
Chapter Five 32
Chapter Six 38
Chapter Seven 43
Chapter Eight 47
Chapter Nine 53
Chapter Ten 57
Chapter Eleven 64
Chapter Twelve 69
Chapter Thirteen 74
PART TWO 77
July 1983 78
Chapter Fourteen 79
Chapter Fifteen 83
Chapter Sixteen 92
Chapter Seventeen 97
Chapter Eighteen 105
Chapter Nineteen 111
PART THREE 114
August 1983 115
Chapter Twenty 116
Chapter Twenty-One 120
Chapter Twenty-Two 125
Chapter Twenty-Three 132
Chapter Twenty-Four 137
Chapter Twenty-Five 145

Chapter Twenty-Six	149
Chapter Twenty-Seven	154
Chapter Twenty-Eight	159
Chapter Twenty-Nine	164
PART FOUR	166
October 1983	167
to June 1988	168
Chapter Thirty	169
Author's Note	171
Acknowledgments	173

PART ONE

June 1983

Chapter One

Lorraine

The craziest thing that has ever happened to me happened on an ordinary summer night. It was the summer of 1983. Ronald Reagan was president. Sally Ride was all over the news. *Flashdance* and *Return of the Jedi* were the big movies. Metallica, one of my favorite bands, released a new album. And, in the middle of all that, this happened in my dull life...

I have to start by telling you where I lived first. I lived in Southwest Philadelphia on Bonnaffon Street, a little street that was sandwiched between Paschall Avenue and Woodland Avenue, or The Avenue, as we called it. The Avenue was where all the shops were in Southwest Philly; the business district, I guess you could call it. I lived with my mother, Sandra Kowalksi, and my grandmother, Joyce Evans. I also have an older brother named Paulie, but he moved out the year before into an apartment in Glenolden to live with his girlfriend Deirdre. Glenolden is a town in Delaware County, or Delco. Delco is the suburbs just outside Southwest Philly.

I just graduated from John Bartram High School the day before. Yeah, just one day earlier, I was getting my high-school diploma. Mom and Grandmom said it was a first. Neither of them finished high school, and Paulie didn't, either. Of course, Mom had to dump all over my accomplishment and say that I finished with a C average, and even a D in some of my classes. Well, I finished high school, which was a hell of a lot more than she did.

A week earlier, I walked out of my job at McDonald's because my manager grabbed my ass while I was working in the drive-through. It wasn't the first time he pulled that crap, either. I remember how pissed off Mom was when I came home that night and told her I quit. She called me a bum and a freeloader, just like my useless father, and good luck getting another job.

My parents split up when I was five. I'd seen my dad three times between the split-up and the start of this story, the last time being when I was fifteen. He was living in a trailer in South Jersey, somewhere in the Pine Barrens, with his girlfriend, a lady named Pauline. He promised to send me money so that I could go to junior college after high school, but he never did.

Grandmom moved in after Dad split to help Mom with taking care of me and Paulie. Grandpop died the year before, so Grandmom sold their house on Wheeler Street and moved in with us. Because Grandmom was on disability, she had lots of time on her hands and could stay home all the time and always be there for us and take care of us. Mom worked ten-hour shifts at X-Mark, a company in Delco that made plastics, so she couldn't be home as much as she wanted to take care of me and Paulie when we were little. But then we had to start taking care of Grandmom because her COPD was starting to get bad. She went on oxygen that year and started wheeling a tank with her everywhere she went. She still smoked, too, which she really shouldn't have done. But she didn't care and said she was going to croak anyway, so she might as well go out the way she pleased.

I was what the snotty West Catholic kids called a burnout. Because I drank and smoked and did a little weed and listened to metal and hung out with JDs. They were nothing to write home about themselves, those West kids. They were stuck up as hell.

Yeah, I liked heavy metal. I liked Ozzy, Van Halen, Metallica, and Journey. Van Halen was my favorite of the bunch. I had posters of them on my bedroom wall. I had a raging crush on Alex Van Halen, their drummer. I thought he was smokin' hot! And I thought it was so awesome that our birthdays were so close. His was May 8th, and mine was May 15th.

Anyway, enough about me, and on with the story. I was sitting around the house watching TV with Grandmom on the night this story started. We were watching *Action News* and laughing at Jim

O'Brien, the weatherman. He was one funny dude. Mom was due home soon. I remember that I was wearing the shirt I bought at the Journey mega concert a week earlier. It was a humongous concert held at JFK Stadium, and they headlined it. John Cougar, The Tubes, Sammy Hagar, and Bryan Adams were there, too. The Tubes opened. It was an awesome show! I went with my friends DeeDee Bower and Michelle Richards. They lived on my street, and while I wasn't real close with them, they said I could tag along. We had a blast!

"Your mother will be home soon," Grandmom said. She said that every day at that time, as if I forgot that this was always the time Mom came home. She smoked a cigarette and let out a raspy laugh at Jim O'Brien throwing magnets shaped like clouds onto the weather map.

"You need to give up smoking, Grandmom," I told her.

"Yeah, I need to do a lot of things," she said. "What *you* need to do is start looking for a job and help your mother out. I don't know why you stormed out of work like you did."

"We've been over this. I told you my manager was a douche."

"He grabbed your ass; so what? You're a cute girl. You should have let him ask you out. That relationship could have led somewhere."

Mom and Grandmom were from a totally different generation, one where men did crap like that to women and got away with it. I didn't even answer her. She just didn't get it.

"Anyway, look at Paulie. He didn't even graduate from high school and still was able to get a steady job at that auto-parts place. Him and Deidre are doing okay in Delco. She's going to hairdressing school and will probably be working in a salon in another year." Mom and Grandmom thought Paulie was perfect. I would get so sick of hearing about him and how he did no wrong. Again, I didn't answer her.

As *Action New*s ended, I heard Mom's '73 Nova pull up in front of the house. A minute later she was in the door. For forty-four years old, she looked like hell. She looked closer to sixty, and her raggedy work outfit didn't help matters. Every day she wore a flannel shirt, jeans, and work boots to work. Her long, dark hair, which had a lot of gray in it, was always in a braid that hung down her back, and a bandanna was on top of her head to keep her hair in place. I rarely saw her dressed nice, and I felt bad for her. I knew from old pictures of her that she was a pretty, dark-haired, dark-eyed girl once upon a time, before Dad split and sent her life on a downward spiral.

"Did you look for a job today?" Mom said as a greeting as she pulled off her work boots.

"No," I said.

"Well, you need to get your ass out there and start looking. Apply at places in Delco if you have to. It's not that far away. You can take the trolley and a bus there every day." Every day since I quit McDonald's, she told me this. Her and Grandmom were two broken records.

"Are you still considering Katharine Gibbs?" she asked as she walked into the kitchen to make dinner. Katharine Gibbs was a secretarial school in town on Broad Street. Mom heard about it from a friend and was big on the idea of my going there.

"I dunno. I don't think I'd make a good secretary," I said.

"I think you would. You're an okay typist. You should give it a shot, or else you'll end up like me in some shitty factory." I wanted to tell her that I'd probably end up like her anyway regardless of what I did to improve my life.

A few minutes later, she called out, "Dinner's ready when youse are," as she turned off the crock pot. Me and Grandmom got up and went into the kitchen as Mom ladled beef stew into bowls. I was pretty quiet during dinner as Mom and Grandmom talked. I was thinking about hitting the street corner and then heading up to Titans afterward. Titans was a video arcade on The Avenue. I hung out there almost every night. To this day, I still hear the sounds of Pac-Man, Ms. Pac-Man, Donkey Kong, Q-Bert, Joust, Pole Position, and Centipede in my dreams. I watched a lot of fights and drug deals go down in Titans, too. Yeah, it was that kind of place.

I also liked to hang out on the street corner. My location of choice was Paschall and Bonnaffon, right down the street from my house. The same kids from the neighborhood were always there, drinking Bud and blasting tunes from 94 WYSP from a boombox.

I didn't want to stay with Mom and Grandmom any longer that night, so I shoveled the beef stew down my throat as fast as I could and told them I was going out.

"Yeah, have fun with those losers," Mom called out as I headed for the front door. "You're gonna get knocked up! I'm surprised you haven't by now!" I didn't even say goodbye. As I walked down to the corner, I took my comb out of my back pocket and ran it through my light-brown, shoulder-length, feathered hair. I saw Bobby Murphy, Danny Myers, Joey Mullen, and Nicky Santora already there drinking Bud. "Gimme All Your Lovin'" by ZZ Top was playing on the boombox close by.

"What's up, Lorraine?" Bobby said as I came up to them. I had to admit he was looking foxy in his cutoff, mesh Wildwood '83 shirt. He had a good body for that shirt. He probably bought it when he was down the shore a few weeks ago for Memorial Day weekend. His brown hair was perfectly feathered on either side, and he wore denim shorts, tube socks, and high-topped Nikes. He also wore a gold stud earring in his left ear. He sipped his Bud as he looked over the rim of his can at me. I knew what he was thinking, too. He was a total pervert, to be honest.

"I'm doin' good," I said. "What's goin' on with youse?"

"Nothin' much," Danny said. "We may go cruisin' into Delco tonight, see some friends there. Wanna come?

"No thanks. I wanna go to Titans after this."

"Why? You got someone waitin' up there for you?" Joey asked.

"No, I feel like playin' arcade games. Can't a girl go in there and play arcade games?"

"I dunno, Joe DiGiacomo has a thang for you," Nicky said with a leer. Joe was Titans's owner. He was shifty as hell and someone you took pains to avoid.

"Fuck Joe, he's a scumbag. I wouldn't go anywhere near him." I took the Bud out of Bobby's hand and took a sip. He touched the roach clip I had clipped into my hair. I forgot it was there. "Can I use this for my joint?" he asked.

"No, sorry, I wanna keep it. Darlene Burton made it for me." Darlene was one of the girls in my neighborhood. She was the closest thing to a best friend that I had. I say that because she was my friend when her other best friend wasn't around. Otherwise, she pretty much left me alone.

"I'll give you a beer if you want one," he said,

"No, it's all right. I just needed to wet my whistle," I said as I handed it back to him,

"That's probably not all that's wet," Nicky said, and the others laughed.

"You're disgusting! The fuck's the matter with you?" I screeched.

"Aww, Lor, don't be mad," Nicky said. "You know I'm just messin' with ya, right?"

"Well, my work is done here. I'm heading up to Titans," I said as I walked away.

"Suck my dick, Kowalski!" Danny yelled.

"In your dreams, babe!" I yelled back. They laughed as I kept walking back up my street towards The Avenue. What a bunch of losers, and yeah, Mom was right: it was a wonder that none of them had knocked me up. I hadn't dated many guys in my neighborhood, only about three or so, and those relationships went nowhere. So many losers where I lived. Where were the decent guys? And where were the decent friends? I was friendly with a few kids in my neighborhood, but I didn't have a best friend. Darlene was only my best friend when it was convenient for her, and I know she sure as hell wasn't thinking about me while she was down the shore hanging out with other people.

While I was thinking about it, I wondered where there was a decent life. I had no goals or dreams. I would probably turn out like Grandmom or Mom and get a job at X-Mark or some other factory and eventually start wheeling around an oxygen tank myself and living in Southwest Philly forever. Dreams of good relationships and good jobs were for the upper-class West Catholic kids, not lower-class Bartram kids like me. We didn't have any advantages. Life gave us what it gave us, and we tried to make the best of it.

I crossed The Avenue and walked down to Titans. Before I even walked through the door, I could hear "Separate Ways" by Journey blasting from the jukebox and the noise from all the people inside the arcade. I walked into a cloud of cigarette smoke and the faint smell of weed. I hoped the cops didn't come along and bust us all if they smelled the weed.

The place had no lights; all the light was from the arcade machines, and they were in full swing. Kids were crowded around, all of them cheering and yelling. One kid dressed just like Steve Perry in a checkerboard shirt and jeans was yelling happily as he got the high score on Pole Position while a guy in a Grab a Heiny shirt yelled in disappointment as his friend beat him at Joust.

A lot of people wore concert shirts like mine from bands like Ozzy, Black Sabbath, Metallica, and Megadeath. Some girls wore cutoff sweatshirts like Jennifer Beals in *Flashdance*. I saw it the weekend before at a cinema in town with Darlene, right before she split for the shore.

There were also a few people wearing Sixers shirts. They won the championship a few weeks earlier, and there was a lot of celebrating. A lot of kids in Bartram cut school to go to the parade in Center City. Not me, though.

Guys and girls both wore feathered hair. Some guys wore hair that was long in the back and short in the front. It was a very new, hip hairstyle. Other guys went for the Steve Perry look with the longish, straight, flat hair. The girls, like me, aimed to get their feathers as big and fluffy as possible. Guys and girls carried combs with long handles in their back pockets because you always had to keep your 'do looking good.

I walked to the attendant's window and bought $5 in quarters. That was all the money Mom was giving me for the week for Titans, and I decided to blow it all at once. I looked for Joe but didn't see him. As I said, he was the owner of Titans and a huge creep.

I walked over to the Donkey Kong machine after some girls were finished with it and dropped in my quarter. I was playing and minding my own business when I sensed someone standing next to me. I didn't have to look up to see who it was.

"Looorrrrr," I heard Joe slur in my ear. "Good to see you."

Fuck, I thought. I kept playing as if nothing was wrong. "Yeah, Joe, good to see you, too."

"I'm glad to hear you're legal now. Your birthday was last month, right?"

"Yep," I said, not missing a beat with my game.

He leaned in closer, his cologne filling my nostrils. "My girlfriend split a few months ago. I'm still available. Let's make it official. I wanna take you to my crib in Springfield. I'm moving up in the world."

Springfield is a town in Delco. It was rich, from what I'd heard. I observed him from the corner of my eye. He wore a maroon shirt half-unbuttoned that showed off his hairy chest and a gold Miraculous Medal. His short black hair was perfectly feathered, and I didn't have to see him from the back to know that his black dress pants were extra tight around his rear end. The guy was a huge sleaze.

Fortunately, this was when GAME OVER flashed up, giving me a legit excuse to cut out of there. "Sorry, Joe, not interested," I told him.

He looked as if someone just shot him. "Whadaya mean? Jesus Christ, any chick here would kill to hook up with me, and you're turning me down? Do you want to shack up with some Southwest Philly loser? Is that what you want?"

"What I want is none of your business," I snapped as I walked away. "Game over, Joe. Bye!"

"Cunt," he snapped in disgust. I laughed. I planned on staying until all my quarters were used up, but I realized it would be a lot smarter to leave Titans now. I didn't know what I would do with the rest of my night. It was only around seven-thirty, and there was still plenty of daylight. It seemed a shame to go home so soon. Maybe I should ask around and see if anyone was going to throw a party that night and if I could come. I could be in the mood for liquor, a keg, and maybe some weed.

AC/DC's new song "Flick of the Switch" came on the jukebox, and I quietly sang along to it as I walked out of Titans and planned what I was going to do next. Then I saw something that stopped me dead in my tracks: parked just a block away was a white 1983 BMW 320i, the kind of car you never see in Southwest Philly. It looked so out of place that I had to gawk at it. What the hell was a car like that doing there? My first thought was that it was either stolen or a drug dealer's car. I knew it wasn't Joe's car because he drove a Trans Am.

My curiosity was killing me, so I walked over to the Beamer to get a look at the driver. It was a girl who looked to be my age. She wore a pearl necklace and matching pearl studs; her jewelry looked real, too. A white sweater was tied around her shoulders, and she wore a pink alligator shirt. Her hair, which was held in place with a pink ribbon hairband, was very straight, curled under at the ends, and came to her shoulders, and she wore straight, flat little bangs. Her makeup was minimal: all she wore was mascara and sheer pink lip gloss.

No one in Southwest Philly had such a rich, preppy, clean, and innocent look. She obviously wasn't from the neighborhood; how had she wound up here? But what shocked me the most about her wasn't her unusual outfit or her fancy car but her face! I felt as if I was staring in a mirror because me and this girl looked identical! Even down to our light-brown hair and hazel eyes! Every single detail matched!

She obviously noticed this, too, because she stared at me the same way I was staring at her. Then she spoke, in a funny kind of low, quiet way that sounded as if she was speaking through clenched teeth, so very different from the Southwest Philly accent that was the only accent I'd ever heard. "Hello to you. I've finally met my doppelganger."

Chapter Two

Daven

I was a long way from my home in Haverford, in more ways than one. How had I wound up in this godforsaken neighborhood and come face-to-face with my doppelganger, no less?!

Well, the story goes as follows. I was driving home from my friend Rebecca "Bex" Fowler's townhouse in Society Hill. Bex was a friend of mine from Baldwin. I had gone to her place for lunch that afternoon; her best friend, Jensen Carmody, joined us. We had "real" Bloodies with vodka, even though we told Bex's parents they would be virgin drinks! I only had one, as I would be driving myself home. After several hours, our date ended, and I headed home to Haverford.

I encountered an accident on Interstate 95. My exit, Route 420, wasn't for a few more miles, but I didn't feel like sitting in that mess. I hopped off at the Island Avenue exit, the exit closest to me; I assumed I could backtrack home from there. I drove a few miles up that road into a neighborhood I had never been in before and was more than a little afraid of and made a right onto Woodland Avenue. Warning bells rang throughout my head as I became increasingly frightened. I heard Daddy, who always cautioned me to use common sense in such situations, demanding that I abort the mission!

I made a blatant U-turn in the middle of the street, not caring if a cop ticketed me for it. I would have welcomed a cop's appearance at that juncture. I couldn't drive in my nervous state, so I pulled alongside the curb about a block down from a video arcade called Titans, according to the bright yellow sign bearing this information on the front of the building. I popped open the glove compartment, pulled out a road map, and tried to pinpoint my location on it. I saw that I wasn't too far from U.S. Route 13, and that if I could get on it and follow it for a few miles, it would take me right into Route 420, which would put me on Route 320, which would put me on Lancaster Avenue and the path home.

I kept the map unfolded on the passenger's seat and was about to start my car and take off when someone approached me and peered inside. She was a girl my age with feathered hair adorned with a long, feathery clip. She wore a three-quarter-sleeved shirt with the word JOURNEY splashed across the front and tight designer jeans stuffed into a pair of high-topped Nike sneakers. Her face, with its eyes rimmed in black eyeliner, was full of kindness and concern. She was the most reassuring person I had encountered, and I felt much better when I saw her.

I stared at her, and not just because of the unusual way she was dressed but also because she looked identical to me! The same hair and eye color, the same facial features, everything! It was like staring into a mirror! She must have realized this, too, because she stared back at me with the same expression of shock. "Hello to you. I've finally met my doppelganger," I said to her.

"This is freaky," the girl said in a guttural accent that I had never heard spoken on the Main Line.

We stared at each other for another minute, not knowing what to make of this. I thought I had gone crazy; perhaps she thought the same about herself. Indeed, we were imagining this. It was some weird dream, right? Then, I remembered my dilemma and confessed to her, "I don't know where I am."

"Well," she replied, "you're in Southwest Philadelphia. Southwest Philly to us locals. I take it you're lost?"

"Yes. I'm trying to get to Route 13. I was on 95 and had to hop off because of an accident. That's how I wound up here. I need to take 13 to Route 420."

"That's not too hard. You want to keep driving straight, in the direction you're facing. You'll then leave Philly and be in Darby; this street will change names and become Main Street. You'll bump into

13 soon enough. You'll know it because you'll see a big church called Blessed Virgin Mary at the intersection. Make a left there and follow the signs to stay on 13. You'll have to drive about three or four miles or so down 13 until you bump into 420, and then you make a right.

"But the road's gonna split not long after you turn at BVM, so you want to make sure you bear left at the split. A lot of people get confused and bear right, although if you went that way, you'd still bump into 420."

I struggled to remember all that. "Thank you," I said. She was about to walk away when an idea hit me. "Look, I know we've known each other for merely five minutes, but would you like to come home with me? I promise I won't bite, and I want to get to know my identical twin. I have a nice house in Haverford. I think you'll like it."

She was silent for a few seconds, debating whether to accept my offer. "Where's Haverford?" she asked, to my surprise. I thought everyone knew where Haverford was.

"On the Main Line," I replied.

"Oh, where the rich people live?" she asked.

I laughed. "Yes, where the rich people live."

"Okay, sure. I'll navigate you in case my directions screwed you up. Let me call my mom and let her know I'll be out late, okay?" I assented, and she walked to a nearby payphone. A few minutes later, she was back and hopped into my car.

"My name is Lorraine Kowalski," she said, as she plopped into the seat.

I extended my hand to shake hers. "Daven Eleanor Barrett," I replied. "It's wonderful to meet you!"

"Same here."

I popped Genesis's album *Abacab* into the tape deck. "Do you like Genesis?" I asked her as I put the car in gear and pulled away from the curb, the "Abacab " opening notes drifting from the stereo.

"Yeah, they're okay," she said. "I like rock and heavy metal. Journey, Ozzy, Metallica, and Van Halen are my favorites."

"I've heard of some of those bands. Genesis is my favorite because their music is good. But also, because they met in prep school, which is cool because my brother and I went to prep school, too."

"What's a prep school?" she asked, and I tried not to laugh. This Lorraine Kowalski was from a world much different from mine, and I didn't want to make her feel bad for that. "It's a private high school that prepares you for college, hence the name," I explained. "I went to the Baldwin School in Bryn Mawr, and my brother went to the Haverford School in Haverford. Both schools are close to where we live."

"Oh, well, I went to John Bartram High School," Lorraine said. "It's just a regular public school in Southwest Philly. It didn't exactly prepare me for college, though. My grades weren't that great. My mom wants me to go to secretarial school, but I'm not so sure about it."

"I'm going to Vassar College in the fall and will major in art history. It's in Poughkeepsie, New York, which is close to Manhattan. Clay – my brother–will be a senior at Cornell University, which is also in New York, in a town called Ithaca. He and I will be close to each other. Mummy and Daddy wanted that. They didn't like sending me away alone so far from home. My attending Vassar was their idea, even though I would have been perfectly happy at either Oberlin or Barnard, which are the other schools that accepted me. It's important to them that I go to a school close to Clay's for my protection."

"I graduated from Bartram yesterday," Lorraine said.

"Really?" I gasped. "That's a coincidence because I graduated yesterday from Baldwin! We are a lot alike!" After a few minutes, we came to the church she had mentioned, and she directed me to make a left there. She made sure I followed the signs and stayed on Route 13. The neighborhood looked better in this neck of the woods. It wasn't exactly ritzy, but neither did it look as seedy as where we had been.

We continued to talk as we drove on. "Tell me about your family," I said.

"I live with my mom and my grandmom. I have an older brother named Paulie, who is twenty. He moved out last year to live with his girlfriend Deirdre. They live close to here." With a wave of her hand, she indicated the area we were driving through. "My dad split when I was five. I haven't seen him in a few years."

"Where in Southwest Philly do you live?"

"On Bonnaffon Street, about two blocks from the Titans arcade."

"Well, as I said, I live in Haverford, a town on the Main Line. My home is called Arnant. My great-great-grandfather Edwin Francis Barrett built it around the turn of the century. Great-Great-Grandpa Edwin made his fortune in the Pennsylvania Railroad as an executive. We're lucky that we still have that money. Daddy is on the boards of directors of many companies in Philadelphia and works as a stockbroker and a financial advisor. Mummy is active in the Junior League."

"Is that a company or something?" Lorraine asked.

I laughed. "No, it's a volunteer organization comprised of women."

"My mom works at a plastics factory called X-Mark. It's in Darby. She's a machine operator. I have no idea where my dad works, or even if he works. He lives in the Jersey Pine Barrens with his girlfriend."

After Lorraine finished talking, she fell silent and looked out the car window at the scenery. I could tell she was overwhelmed by a world as alien to her as hers was to me, and she struggled to process it. My parents disparaged working-class people. They said it was their fault they were disadvantaged, and that they could improve their lot by pulling themselves up by their bootstraps as our ancestors had done way back. I told them it wasn't that easy, that a lot of it depended on life chances and access to opportunity. But my parents wouldn't buy that. You couldn't tell them anything.

I stopped the Genesis tape and told Lorraine she could put what she wanted on the radio. She tuned into a rock station, and The Tubes's song "She's a Beauty" came on.

"I saw these guys at the big Journey concert last week," she told me. "They opened for them."

"Oh? Is that where you got that shirt you're wearing?"

"Yeah."

I hadn't even known this girl for an hour, yet I liked her already. There was something simple and candid and open about her. She seemed to be devoid of deceit and hubris. Not only because she was from humble means but also because it didn't seem to be in her nature to be a liar or a braggart.

Soon we were turning onto Lancaster Avenue. My home wasn't too far away. "We're in luck," I told Lorraine. "My parents left this morning to spend the summer at the shore, in Longport, and Clay is in Europe until the middle of August on a study-abroad program. My parents wanted me to stay in Longport with them, but I wanted peace and asked them to let me stay home alone for the summer. Last year was busy: I went to finishing school in Switzerland, attended two important balls, took my SATs multiple times, and completed many college interviews. This is the first chance I've had to catch my breath. The staff will be off for a few days, and the house will be all ours."

I turned off Lancaster Avenue and drove the remaining mile to Arnant. I punched the code into the gate and swung onto the curved driveway in front of the house. I shut off the car and turned to look at Lorraine, who looked confounded.

Chapter Three

Lorraine

Okay, as a rule, I didn't go around accepting rides from strangers. I knew better than to do that. But I couldn't pass up an opportunity to go off with my identical twin. It was the freakiest thing I'd ever seen in my life. I called Mom and told her I was going to hang out with Dee Dee and Michelle and that I would be home kind of late. Now that I'm eighteen, I don't have a curfew anymore.

I was blown away by what Daven told me about herself. When she talked about Vassar and Cornell and Baldwin and the Haverford School, I never heard of those places. And her parents didn't work, or at least, they didn't work at jobs like my mother and Paulie and my friends' parents worked at. And when she told me about her parents spending all summer at their house down the shore, and her brother spending all summer in Europe, that blew my mind. Nobody I knew had the money to do those things. I could count on the fingers of one hand the number of times in my life that I stayed down the shore for more than one day. And it was always at some dinky motel in Wildwood. And Wildwood was the farthest I'd ever been in my life. People like her, who traveled around the world and spent entire summers down the shore, didn't exist in my world.

But the biggest shock of all came when we got to her house. Or, I should say, her mansion. Jesus! I never saw a place like that! It seemed to stretch for miles in either direction. It was made out of gray stone and had an arched entryway that led onto a big front porch. The door was a big wooden door, and the window in it was made out of diamond-shaped pieces of glass. There were peaks with windows all along the roof, and a few chimneys and a patio or two as well.

We pulled off the road and drove right onto a driveway that curved around a gray stone fountain. I didn't know what to think. I heard of places like this and seen them on TV, but I never thought I'd actually set foot in one. My row house on Bonnaffon Street was a shack compared to this house. It really was.

We got out of the car and walked to the front door. Daven punched a code into a keypad next to it, and the door opened. I followed her in. We were in a foyer with polished marble floors, and in the center was a staircase that curved up to the second floor. It was just like the one in *Gone with the Wind*, that staircase at Twelve Oaks that Scarlett hid underneath to spy on people. On the walls were oil paintings of people, probably family members from the past, judging by how old they looked. There wasn't much furniture in the foyer, just a chair or two, a credenza, and a few floor lamps. The lamps were already lit when we walked in.

"Welcome to Arnant! I think it's the most beautiful home in the world! It was featured in *Town and Country* in an article about the Main Line last year. Come on." Daven took me by the hand, and we ran up the staircase together. We made a left down the hallway and walked past lots of paintings and a few pieces of furniture before we got to her bedroom, which was the last door on the left. Or, I should say, doors, because they were double doors. White with gold trim and shiny gold doorknobs. She pushed them open.

I probably don't have to tell you that her bedroom was beautiful! It was the kind of bedroom I always dreamed of having, instead of the bedroom I actually had, which overlooked the back alley and had thin walls through which I could hear Grandmom's snoring and raspy coughing and farting every night. This bedroom was fit for royalty.

Centered on the back wall was a queen-sized, canopied bed with a pink comforter and frilly pink pillow shams. The headboard was white wood carved in the shape of hearts. On either side of the bed were white nightstands. Off to the side was a huge white dresser and a white vanity table. On the other side of the room was a white sofa with pink cushions, a white coffee table with some magazines on it, and two cushioned pink chairs. On the side of the room with the dresser were two doors. I assumed one was a bathroom, and the other a closet.

The wallpaper was pink with small white roses, and the thick shag rug was pink, too. It was a total girl's bedroom.

"Have a seat," Daven said, waving me into one of the chairs. She walked over to the stereo and took out an album from the cabinet underneath it. The album was called *Murmur*, and it was from a band called R.E.M. I'd never heard of them. She put it onto the turntable, and a bouncy song called "Radio Free Europe" started to play. She then left to go get food and drinks from the kitchen, and while she was gone, I did some exploring. I found that those two doors were indeed a bathroom and a closet, but the closet was a room! I never saw such a thing! It was probably about as big as my bedroom, and it was full of clothes and shoes. She must have had a hundred shoes in there, no lie. She probably owned more clothes and shoes than all the girls in my neighborhood combined!

I wandered around the room and saw a Polaroid of Daven, dressed in a white gown and holding a bouquet of red roses, propped up on her vanity table. I thought it was a prom picture until I saw the caption written underneath it that said "Daven, Baldwin Class of '83, June 10, 1983." Well, well, well, I thought. They wear gowns to their graduation!

On the opposite wall was another picture of Daven, also in a white gown. But this gown was even fancier. It looked as if it was made out of satin and had a very full skirt. She wore long white gloves that came up past her elbows and held a bouquet of red and pink roses with gold ribbons. This must have been a prom picture, but no, the small gold plate on the bottom of the frame was engraved with the words *28th International Debutante Ball. Daven Eleanor Barrett. December 29th, 1982.* I would have to ask her about this if she didn't bring it up.

I probably don't have to tell you that it was freaky looking at those pictures. They could have been pictures of me.

I went back to my chair and sat and listened to the R.E.M. album while I waited for Daven to return with food. I was starting to get hungry. Then the door opened, and she came through with a silver tray holding a stack of pastries, a pitcher filled with what looked like iced tea, two small bowls of fruit salad, and two empty glasses. She set the tray down on the coffee table and poured iced tea for us. I took a sip. It was mint iced tea and very good!

"I hope you like scones," she said as she placed one on a small china plate and handed it to me. I took a bite, and it had strawberry filling inside. I never had a scone, but this one was pretty tasty.

"This is delicious. Thank you," I said.

"You're welcome. I would have called Consuelo, our head maid, to bring this, but as I said, the staff has off for two weeks. So, I'm fending for myself."

"Aren't you afraid to stay in this huge house all by yourself? What if someone breaks in?" I asked.

She laughed. "Oh, Lorraine, I can tell you're from the city! Only a city person would ask a question like that! This is why I like you already: you are so different from me! Well, to set your mind at ease, we have a good security system here at Arnant, and security guards are constantly monitoring the house through cameras."

"Will you get in trouble for having me here?"

"No, my parents are okay with me bringing people over. And anyway, it's highly unlikely the monitored security system will tell them about you. My parents would only be informed in the case of suspicious activity, like a trespasser or a break-in."

For the first time, I got a good look at her whole outfit. Along with the alligator shirt and the white sweater, she wore mint-green shorts, cuffed white socks, and white Keds. Her pocketbook was sitting on the sofa. It was beige canvas with brown handles and two purple stripes running down the front. A tag with the name L.L. Bean was on the front, too. It looked like an expensive bag. In fact, all her clothes and accessories looked expensive.

She took off her sweater and dropped it next to her pocketbook. The sweater had the initials DBE embroidered on the front. I never saw anybody dress this way. Nobody in my neighborhood wore their initials on their clothes or even dressed in pastels. Kids wore concert shirts, flannel shirts, T-shirts, denim, leather, and Spandex, and that was pretty much it.

She sat on the chair opposite from me and helped herself to a scone and a glass of iced tea. R.E.M. played as we talked. "I couldn't help but notice that picture of you at the debutante ball. What was that?"

"Oh, the deb ball. You know, it's for rich, high-society girls to come out, or to be formally presented to society. It's held in New York City at the Waldorf Astoria Hotel every two years. My parents wanted me to debut as soon as possible after finishing school, and that's what I did. I was in finishing school all last summer, and I debuted last December."

"What's a finishing school?" I asked, my mouth full of scone.

"It's a special school where they teach girls social graces, like how to walk properly, sit properly, set a table, and other such things. I already know a lot of that stuff because it's been drilled into me all my life, but my parents wanted to send me off anyway. I attended the Institut Villa Pierrefeu in Montreaux, Switzerland, which was right near Lake Geneva.

"Oh God, what a time that was to be alive!" she laughed. "We took a day trip to Gstaad and got hopelessly lost while hiking! I never thought we'd see the school again! It was a nice city but full of Eurotrash. Another time, a bunch of us snuck out at night, drove to Geneva in a classmate's car, and bribed the doorman of a dance club to let us in. We snuck back to school a few hours before our morning class. None of us slept that night. I don't think the school ever found out about it, either!"

I laughed, too, at these rich girls' shenanigans and thought that me and Daven weren't all that different. She walked over to another picture on the wall, one I didn't see. She was wearing a white gown in that one, too. Did she wear white gowns for all her pictures?

"Here I am at the Philadelphia Charity Ball. It was held in November, about a month before the New York deb ball. I've been to so many balls in my life. They've become utterly boring to me now."

The more she talked, the more overwhelmed I felt. Girls like her never, ever associated with someone like me, and yet, here I was in her bedroom in a mansion on the Main Line. This had to be a weird dream that I was going to wake up from any minute.

We finished the scones and iced tea and sat there not saying anything, looking around the room and listening to R.E.M. Then, Daven got up, took the needle off the record, turned off the record player, and walked to one of the windows. It had a window seat covered in pink cushions, and she sat on it and looked out into the night. The room was so quiet; so was outside. I didn't hear a sound. Unlike my neighborhood, where at any given moment, you could hear kids talking loudly on the corner, people arguing, babies and little kids crying, and screeching cats.

It was starting to feel awkward, like maybe I should say something, but I didn't know what. Then Daven piped up with, "Lorraine, I have a plan for us. I know it's risky and daring, but I want to do it. I want to switch identities. For just this summer, you be me, and I'll be you. How about it?"

Chapter Four

Daven

Proposing to switch identities for the summer was the riskiest idea I had ever had. But the more I looked at Lorraine and me, the more the idea cried out to come to fruition.

I was tired of my pampered yet utterly confining and restricting life. I wanted to live as Lorraine did, with almost unlimited freedom, even if that freedom was steeped in poverty.

And I wanted Lorraine to taste the good life of Main Line high-WASP society. It was probably the only taste she would ever get of it, too. Lord knew she had her fill of poverty.

Lorraine was aghast, but I continued. "The conditions are perfect to do this. My family will be gone for the next two and a half months, so we won't have to worry about them noticing anything unusual. Neither of us has a boyfriend, so that's one less complication there as well. I don't have any friends that I'm particularly close to, and I get the feeling you don't, either. You have your mom and your grandmom to deceive, but I think we can get this past them if we try hard enough.

"I also feel that you would love to see how the other half lives. Well, so would I! You may think I'm some spoiled little rich girl who leads a perfect life. I'm going to tell you that I'm not. My life has always been sheltered. I've never had to make decisions or do major things for myself or provide for myself; my parents have always done that for me.

"My parents fear me associating with people who can hurt me or take advantage of me because of my wealth and my social status, which is why they feel the need to protect me from the evil in the world. That they're letting me stay home alone all summer is a miracle, but I assume by this point in my life they trust me to stay out of trouble.

"I've never really lived. Yes, I've done lots of exciting things in my life, like traveling and attending balls and going to the best schools, but none of it was done at my behest. Switching identities will be the first major decision I've ever made, and it will give me a chance to see what your life is like.

"And now you can really feel sorry for me when I tell you that I have no friends I've made on my own, without my parents' intercession. My friends are the kids of my parents' friends, or the kids of people they're acquainted with. My parents need to evaluate and select my friends, and it goes back to their overprotectiveness. You're the first friend I've chosen on my own."

"This sounds so risky," Lorraine said. "Could we really pull it off?"

"Yes, we can! As I said, many of the people close to us are either absent or are pretty much tuned out, like your mom and your grandmom. And the lack of boyfriends and best friends means that there are fewer people to navigate around. Also, wouldn't you love to live my life? Complete with balls, polo matches, designer clothes, lots of spending money, and staff to wait on you twenty-four/seven? Think how exciting that would be for you!"

"And I would love to live your life! I really would!" I finished breathlessly.

"But I'm piss broke and live like shit!" Lorraine said. "How could that possibly be fun for you? It's way below your standard of living."

I laughed. "That may be true, but your life has something all my money can't buy: freedom. You can do as you please and aren't dependent on a trust fund that can be cut off if you commit the slightest infraction. You don't have to walk tightropes that, if you fall off them, will sully your family both in high society and in the public eye. You can live almost any way you choose. I want a taste of that life, even for a summer."

"Okay, but now that you've told me that even the slightest infraction will make your parents cut off your trust fund, then why do you want to do this identity switch? Aren't you afraid of the trouble you'll get into, and the loss of your trust fund?"

"We'll be careful, and we'll plan for it properly. Besides, it'll only be for the summer; no one will catch onto us in that brief amount of time."

"Exactly what's the timeframe?" she asked. I jumped up, walked over to my desk, and took a small calendar off it. I flipped through the summer months to the crucial late August days that preceded my departure to Vassar.

"See here," I showed her as I pointed to the annotated August twenty-first. "This is the day I drive up to Vassar. It's freshman move-in day. A good day to end the identity switch would be the day before, Saturday the twentieth. It'll only be for about two months. I say we do it!"

"But we have no idea how to be each other!" she said. "I don't know how to play polo and eat caviar and do all the things that rich people do, and you don't know how to fistfight, drink at keggers, and jam to metal like a poor person like me does.

"Don't worry, we'll have a boot camp!" I laughed.

"Boot camp?"

"Yes, boot camp! Starting tomorrow, we'll practice being each other. I'll teach you all the things you need to know to move in high society, and you'll teach me all I need to know about being a Southwest Philly chick! It'll be totally awesome! And the best part about it will be that we'll have the house and the grounds all to ourselves.

"If we work hard and fast enough, by this time next week, we'll each have learned what we'll need to know to act like the other. Lorraine, this is going to be so much fun!"

"I dunno, it sounds pretty risky," she demurred.

"Please, Lorraine, this is a huge opportunity for both of us! Please say you'll do it." I had never wanted anything more in my life. I wanted to be her so badly. I wanted to know how lower-income people lived. Their lives seemed so simple and uncomplicated. They were very direct, open, and didn't play scheming, Machiavellian games. But I also wanted her to live my life so she could discover that a much better world loomed beyond Southwest Philly, and that she could be a part of it—if only for a short time.

Lorraine rose and paced the room. Then she let out a big gasp and said, "Okay, let's do it. But we have to make sure we're really thorough. We have to learn as much as we can about each other during boot camp. And the identity switch has to be over by the end of summer."

I squealed with glee and hugged her. "Oh, thank you, Lorraine! We're going to have the time of our lives, wait and see!"

She hugged me back. I loved this girl. I had already considered her my best friend and hoped she felt the same about me. I knew God had a reason for causing the accident on 95, directing me to get off at Island Avenue, and getting me lost in Southwest Philly: all those things were put in motion to lead me to Lorraine.

"Let's start boot camp now!" I said. I extracted a photo album from my bookcase, and we sat on the floor and opened it. "Here is Daddy, Clayton Frederick Barrett, Jr. He goes by the name Clay. He's always lived on the Main Line, as have my family going back to my great-great-grandfather Edwin. Daddy attended The Haverford School, the same as my brother Clay, and Princeton University. His hobbies are playing polo, playing squash, and drinking martinis, sometimes getting loaded off the martinis," I added with a giggle.

"This is Mummy, Edith Margaret Darnley Barrett. She's called Pepper. She attended Baldwin and Sarah Lawrence and comes from Main Line stock, the same as Daddy. As I mentioned, she's very active in the Junior League and lends a hand at other charitable endeavors when not busy playing tennis at the Merion Cricket Club.

"This charmer here is my brother, Clayton Frederick Barrett, III. As I mentioned, he attended The Haverford School and is enrolled at Cornell. His only hobbies are hanging out with his frat-boy friends, chasing girls, and squandering his trust fund."

I showed her pictures of Rebecca Fowler and Jensen Carmody and gave her a bio for each. Fortunately, since I didn't have too many friends, she didn't have to remember details for very many people. After we finished looking through the album, she said, "I hope I remember all this."

"Don't worry," I laughed, "we'll have a refresher course, and we'll each take lots of notes."

"When I come tomorrow, I'll be sure to bring my photo album with pictures of my family," she said.

"Great! I look forward to seeing it. I'll be right back." I left my room, walked down to the first floor, and located one of our china cabinets. I loaded several pieces of glassware, flatware, a few plates, and a linen napkin onto a silver tray and returned them to my room. I cleared off my vanity table and used these items to set up a formal dinner table. I sat Lorraine in front of it.

"Forks on the left, knife and spoons on the right. Butter plate and butter knife up on the left; water goblet, champagne flute, and wine glass up on the right. You don't eat off that plate; it's called a service plate. Your appetizer and your soup or salad are placed directly on top of that plate. When your entrée comes, the service plate is taken away, and your entrée is put in its place.

"There are three forks here. The first fork on the outside is for the salad, the second for the fish course, and the third for the entrée. Then over here is the dinner fork, the soup spoon, and the fruit spoon. A good way to remember which utensils to use and when is to start from the outside and work your way in as each course comes.

"You place the utensils in different ways during and after eating. Placing the fork and knife horizontally and facing to the right means you're finished and liked it. Putting them facing up in an inverted V means you're taking a break. Crisscrossing them in a T means you're ready for the next course."

"As soon as you sit down, put your napkin in your lap." I demonstrated this for her as she watched. "Also, when you come to the table, the man you came with will pull your seat out for you and help you slide in. Then the men at the table will sit. If you get up from the table to, say, use the bathroom, the men will get up. Leave your napkin slightly folded and to the right of your plate. When you come back, they'll get up again and sit down when you do."

Lorraine laughed. "That's so much to remember just to eat dinner! I've never been given lots of forks, cups, and plates or ever had a guy pull out a chair for me."

"This will be a wonderful learning experience for you! Now, let's go through it again." I drilled her on the items and had her repeat back to me what each was and when it was to be used. With just a few hints from me, she remembered everything almost perfectly.

I told her to stand so I could show her how to properly sit in a chair. "Stand in front of the chair with your knees together. Ease down gently while keeping your arms straight. Try not to use them for balance. Use your hands to smooth down your skirt in the back as you're sitting down. Pretend you're wearing one and smooth it down. That's it. Once you're down, keep one foot flat on the floor while you cross the other behind it at the ankle. Sit up straight in the center of the chair and don't lean back on it. There! You have it!"

We ran through the chair part a few more times, then I drilled her again on the tableware. She learned most of the lesson quickly.

"There's something else we have to think about," she said. "The way we talk!"

I hadn't realized that. She spoke in a heavy Southwest Philadelphia accent, and I in a Main Line accent. Each of us would have to emulate the other, and it wasn't going to be easy. We spent the next hour on this topic, each of us pronouncing words two different ways. I would have to remember to say "wooder" instead of "water," "gone" instead of "going," "wit" instead of "with." She recited these words, too, enunciating them fully and properly, speaking in the stiff, stilted way in which I had spoken all my life. It wasn't an easy feat for either of us!

It was getting late, close to eleven o'clock, and I told Lorraine I would take her home. "Will you be available all week?" I asked her as we sped back to Southwest Philly.

"Yeah. I don't have any plans."

"Good. The boot camp will be held at my place. Tomorrow, I'll come to pick you up around eleven in the morning. Why don't we meet right down from Titans, in the spot where we met tonight? This way, your mom won't question a Beamer coming to your house."

"Sounds good."

"We'll do that every day this week: meet near Titans and go to my place from there. This is going to be so much fun!"

We drove some more, and then I pulled over to the side of the road and said to her, "Hey, I want to thank you for helping me tonight when I was in Southwest Philly. I was so scared. You have no idea how kind you were to me."

"You're welcome," Lorraine said with a smile. "I'm glad I met you. I really am."

"And I'm glad I met you."

I pulled back onto the road and tuned the radio to 98 WCAU, the local pop station. "Too Shy" by Kajagoogoo came on as we drove back to Southwest Philly in silence thinking about the deception we were about to enact and wondering how credible of a job we would do.

Chapter Five

Lorraine

It was close to midnight when Daven dropped me off at exactly where we met earlier that night just down from Titans. It would have been too hard to explain to Mom and Grandmom why a Beamer was stopping at the house, plus they didn't know I had gone out with Daven and not DeeDee and Michelle, so I asked Daven to drop me off at Titans. I walked the two blocks to my house and saw that the living room was dark and the TV on. I knew at least Mom was still up. Sure enough, the front door was unlocked, and I let myself in.

She didn't ask me where I was all night. "Grandmom's in bed. Don't wake her up," she said as a greeting, not taking her eyes off of *Saturday Night Live*.

"Okay, I won't. Goodnight." I ran up to my bedroom. Grandmom was in the master bedroom sound asleep. Just like she did every night, she snored, coughed, and farted as she slept. Her ass was stinking up the whole second floor, so I shut her door and sprayed Lysol in my room, the hallway, and Mom's room. Mom's room used to be Paulie's room before he moved out. For years Mom slept on the sofa bed in the living room while he was in that room. Grandmom was in the master bedroom since she moved in years ago. I guess Mom felt it was the least she could do: give Grandmom the master bedroom as thanks for moving in to help raise us.

I went to my room, flopped on my bed, and pondered everything that happened that day. I looked at the posters on my wall and the one of Alex Van Halen pounding away on his drum kit.

"What should I do, Alex?" I asked him, as if he could answer me. My eyes traveled around my bedroom, which was full of dilapidated old furniture. All the furniture in the house was used. People either gave it to us, or we bought it at the thrift store or trash-picked it. The nicest things in my room, which I bought on my own, were a few dolls and stuffed animals, a full-length mirror, and a big jewelry box.

My cap and gown hung from a hook on my closet door, and the cards I got for graduation stood on top of my bureau. My family didn't make a big deal out of my graduation. We – me, Mom, Grandmom, Paulie, and Deirdre – went to an Italian restaurant in Delco called Trieste for dinner. It's close to where Paulie and Deirdre live. Then we came home, and that was that.

I had all of Van Halen's albums, from their first album, *Van Halen*, to the newest one, *Diver Down*, which came out the year before. I put *Van Halen* on my record player, and "Runnin' with the Devil" played, followed by "Eruption." "Eruption" is a kick-ass Eddie Van Halen masterpiece. I was tempted to learn to play guitar just so I could learn to play that song, but I was too lazy. I started thinking how sorry I was that I didn't live in California so that I could have went to the US Festival and seen all the metal bands that performed there, including Van Halen. Stevie Nicks was there, too, and I wish I could have seen her. In fact, she was due to come to Philly in a few weeks, but tickets sold out before I could buy one.

As Eddie Van Halen tore up that guitar, I started to gather up the stuff I would need for the boot camp. I got a tote bag from my closet and packed it with some cassette tapes, a few issues of *Hit Parader,* a photo album that had Polaroids of my family members and a few of my friends, a notebook and pen, and a pimple ball. I hung the tote bag on the knob of my bedroom door so I would remember to take it with me the next morning.

I listened to Van Halen for a little while longer, turned off my record player, and closed my eyes. I had no idea what the next day would bring and didn't think I would be able to fall asleep, I was so nervous. But I did, and I didn't crack my eyes open again until around eight the next morning.

v

Since it was Sunday, Mom was off. Me, her, and Grandmom went to Mass at St. Clement's, our parish church. I went to St. Clement's grade school until I was in second grade, which was when Dad stopped sending us money. Then me and Paulie were taken out and sent to Patterson, which is a public grade school. I liked St. Clement's. Perhaps if I went to Catholic school for all my school years, I would have come out a smarter person. Maybe even almost as smart as Daven.

After Mass, they said they were going to visit a friend who lived in another part of Southwest Philly. They asked me if I wanted to come, but I said no, of course. I told them I wanted to go home instead, so I walked back there, grabbed the tote bag I prepared the night before, and headed up to The Avenue. I left a note for them telling them I was going to be at Titans and hanging out with friends for the rest of the day.

I saw Daven as she pulled up to the curb a little way down from Titans. As soon as I jumped into the Beamer, we took off. Today she wore a sleeveless white blouse, pleated khaki shorts, and white sneakers with a blue U-shaped design on them that I later learned were called Tretorns. She wore her hair in a ponytail, and in the back seat was the same pocketbook she carried yesterday. I wore a pink terrycloth romper, a painter's cap, and high-topped sneakers with sweat socks.

She easily navigated up to Route 13 without my help and sped back to Haverford. I turned on the radio. It was set to 98 WCAU and played Stevie Nicks's new song "Stand Back." It was my favorite song of hers.

"You know," she said as we drove, "This will be just like *Pygmalion*. I'll be the Professor Higgins to your Eliza Doolittle."

"Um...what does that mean?" I asked.

She laughed, but in a nice way. "It's the name of a play where Professor Higgins finds this girl from the lower class and turns her into a lady." Then she looked embarrassed and said, "Please don't take that the wrong way. I didn't mean to imply that you're lower class."

I laughed. "No hard feelings. I know what you mean. It's cool."

She smiled. "But the transformation works both ways, and you'll be my Professor Higgins, just as I'll be yours."

When we got to Arnant, we went right up to her bedroom. I set down my tote bag. "Today, you'll learn some stuff about me," I said.

"Terrific!" she said. "Let me fix lunch for us. I'll be back." A few minutes later, she came back with a tray of tuna sandwiches and a pitcher of iced tea and set it on the coffee table. I didn't realize how hungry I was as I chomped into one of the sandwiches. She turned on her stereo, and "What a Feeling" by Irene Cara came on. It was the theme song from *Flashdance*.

As we ate, I took the stuff out of my tote bag and spread it on the floor. "This is what you need to know to be me," I said. "These are cassettes of the albums of my favorite bands, a few *Hit Parader* magazines, a photo album with pictures of my family and friends, and a pimple ball."

Daven picked up the pimple ball and stared at it as if she never saw one before; she probably hadn't. "This is a pimple ball?"

"Yes."

"What do you do with it?"

"You play with it. Usually, you use it for stickball, but you can toss it and bounce it against walls, which is what I do with it. All the kids in Southwest Philly play with them."

She picked up one of the *Hit Parader*s, the one with David Lee Roth on the cover. "Who's this fellow?" she asked.

"David Lee Roth. He's the lead singer of Van Halen, one of my favorite bands. I have some of their cassettes here for us to listen to." She looked through the magazine, and I said to her, "Why don't you spend some time reading that? Get familiar with some rock bands."

She got up, walked over to the bookcase, took two thick books out of it, and brought them over to me. "Read this one first," she said as she showed me one of the books. "It's the Philadelphia *Social Register* for this year." She flipped to a page and pointed to her family's name. "Here we are listed along with the name of our estate, Arnant." She closed that book, put it down, and showed me the other book. "This is called *The Official Preppy Handbook*. It will teach you a lot about the fashions and the lifestyle of the upper class."

We sat down to read. She read the *Hit Parader* as I read the *Social Register*. It was a confusing book to read, full of all this funny little black print. Some sections of the book were labeled "Married Maidens" and "Dilatory Domiciles." I asked her what those words meant.

"'Married Maidens' is a listing of women that shows both their maiden and married names. Sometimes people forget, so both names are printed as a reminder. 'Dilatory Domiciles' is a list of names of people who didn't return their information cards in time, before the Social Register went to press."

She flipped through *Hit Parader* and pulled out a centerfold of Cheap Trick. "Who are these guys?" she asked.

"That's Cheap Trick. They're not metal. I guess you could call them Punk or New Wave."

"Oh. I think I've heard of them." We kept on reading, and then we stopped, put down the magazines, and picked up the photo albums.

"I know I've shown you these pictures before, but I'll go over them again," she said as she described all her family members and friends to me again. She pointed to a picture of Bex Fowler and Jensen Carmody. "These girls are really the only friends I have. They're best friends who like to keep me around to be an occasional sidekick." She got quiet for a minute. "Lorraine, if we can pull this off, can we be best friends? And even if we can't, can we still be best friends?

This question caught me off-guard. Here was a girl who had everything, and she was asking a poor nobody like me to be her best friend. I didn't know what to say, and it occurred to me that her money could buy her a lot of things, but it couldn't buy her friends.

I gave her a big hug. "Of course. I don't have a best friend, either. You would make the best best friend!" After the hug was over, she wiped away a tear. "Well, now that that's settled, let's get back to boot camp!" We went through all our photo albums again and again drilled each other on our friends' and families' names and details.

After we were done with the albums, we moved on to music. I put a few Van Halen tapes into her tape deck and drilled her on the songs. Then I played them back and had her identify them. I did the same with my Ozzy, Metallica, and Journey tapes. When she had gotten the songs down pat, she put me through the same drill with her tapes from Genesis, R.E.M., and the Go-Go's. We giggled like two little girls when the music session was all over!

While we were doing all this, we took constant notes, because we knew we weren't going to remember all this stuff when the identity switch went live. When we were satisfied that we knew enough about each other's music, we put our tapes away.

"Now what?" I asked.

"Tennis!" she declared.

Chapter Six

Lorraine

We walked outside to the tennis court at the end of her huge back lawn. She carried two rackets and a cylinder of tennis balls. She handed me one of the rackets when we reached the court. I made sure to bring my notebook with me.

"Come here and stand on this line; it's called the baseline," she said as I stood on the line in front of me. "The first thing we'll work on is a serve. Watch how I do it." I watched as she tossed the ball into the air and hit it to the other side of the court. "When you serve the ball, you don't want to use a pushy motion on the ball. You want to rotate your body around and hit the ball as hard as you can." She demonstrated again and then had me do it. The ball hit the net. "Okay, that was good. You just need to give it more power." I did a few more serves before she taught me forehand and backhand moves.

We practiced tennis for an hour and then took a breather by lying side-by-side on the grass and staring up at the sky. We both wore sunglasses and munched on the Tastykakes that I brought and talked about all kinds of stuff. Eventually, our eyes began to feel heavy, and we fell asleep. Two best friends, sleeping on the lawn of a backyard on the Main Line.

Daven

Day two of boot camp began with me showing Lorraine the basics of croquet. After I had explained the game's rules to her, we walked to the end of the back lawn and set up the stakes and wickets. I gave myself an orange mallet and her a green one, and I also gave us balls in coordinating colors.

"The object of the game is to score fourteen wickets," I told her. "You work your way from one end of the field to the other to score them. The order of play is marked on the stake. Orange goes first, and green second, and so on. Every pass through a wicket equals a bonus shot, which means you can go again. When you can't pass through the wicket, the other player goes." We started the game with me going first. I passed my ball through the wicket, and she did likewise with hers.

Eventually, my ball hit hers. I explained that two bonus shots are awarded in this case and demonstrated how to use the ball to hit the opponent's ball out of the way. She took notes of everything I showed her and continued to do so until the end of the game.

She produced a pimple ball from her pocket when that hour was up. "Got a good wall we can use?" she asked. I walked us to a wall along the rear of the house, and she showed me how to bounce the ball back and forth against the wall using her hand as a tennis racket. I tried it, and after several clumsy misses, I got the hang of it. It was a lot of fun!

We took a break for lunch before going up to my bedroom. "Let's see how we do with sizes," I said. "You go into the bathroom and undress. I'll do the same out here. Then we'll try on each other's clothes. We did the outfit switch, and she emerged from the bathroom to see the result. We both laughed, for our clothes fit each other perfectly!

We returned to our original outfits and worked on hair styling. She demonstrated how to feather hair by rolling it onto a curling iron, holding it for several seconds, sliding the curling iron out of the hair, and brushing the resulting roll of hair out into a fluffy wing, using lots of hairspray to hold it. My hair obstinately refused to comply when it was my turn with the curling iron, but I was able to gradually coax it into submission and create a wing that looked like Lorraine's.

She, in turn, replicated my pageboy hairstyle. I showed her how to curl the ends under and use the curling iron to smooth out the bangs. She did a credible job, and I told her she would have no problem replicating it when she had to do it alone.

After our hairstyling class had concluded, I walked over to the record player and put on an album of classical music. "Now I'll show you how to waltz!" I said as the opening notes of "The Blue Danube" by Johann Strauss lilted out of the record player.

"Waltz?!"

"Yes! Come here." She came forward, and I grabbed both her hands. "Put your left hand on my right shoulder and your right hand in the palm of my left hand." She complied as I placed my hand on her right shoulder blade. "Now, you will be the woman, and I the man. This is how you stand with your partner for the waltz. The most basic waltz step is the box step. Watch my feet and follow them." I counted the steps one, two, three. There was a lot of stepping on toes and giggling, which necessitated repeated attempts. We took a few breaks in between for her to take notes.

I started the song over, and we also started our waltz. We moved faster this time, but perhaps it was too soon to accelerate things, for we tripped over each other's feet and fell into a heap on the floor laughing! I laughed because not only did I find the gaffe amusing, but I was also thrilled to have a best friend at last, the best best friend a girl could ever have.

Lorraine

On day three of boot camp, me and Daven watched a little MTV before we got started. As we watched the video for Journey's "Separate Ways," I commented on how much I liked the outfit of the girl in the video. She wore this totally awesome white jacket along with a black skirt and white heels. Daven asked if girls in Southwest Philly dressed that way. I told her some of them did.

"Speaking of Southwest Philly," I added, "let's look at it now." I pulled a Philadelphia street map out of my tote bag and spread it open. I pointed out Southwest Philly and all its important streets and other locations. She took notes on all of it in her notebook.

"This is The Avenue, where we met," I told her as I pointed to Woodland Avenue on the map. "And here is Bonnaffon Street, my street," I told her, pointing to that, too.

After she took more notes, she said, "Let me show you Haverford." She showed me where on the map Arnant was, plus where other places were, like the Haverford train station and Haverford College.

We pointed out to each other other important places as we took more notes in our notebooks. When we had done enough of that, Daven said, "Okay, let's practice our accents." We spent the next two hours drilling each other on our accents again, each of us pronouncing words the way the other would say them.

"Signatures," Daven said. "We should practice each other's signature." She wrote her signature in my notebook, and I wrote mine in hers. Then we copied the signatures as closely as we could a lot of times until we got it right.

"Hopefully, neither of us will have to sign anything, but just in case," she said. We were hungry, so she made turkey sandwiches for us, and we ate them in her room as we watched MTV again. When we finished, she asked, "You're Catholic, right?"

"Yeah."

"You should drill me on the basics of your faith and how I'm supposed to act in a Catholic church. And I can tell you about the basics of Presbyterianism." I told her about the Catholic Church – just what she needed to know, not all the nuts and bolts. I told her Pope John Paul II was the head of the Church, and that Catholics believed in the Holy Trinity and Blessed Mother and the Communion of Saints and the Seven Sacraments. I told her about the Stations of the Cross and the rosary. I showed her how to make the sign of the cross.

"What's the rosary for?" she asked.

"It's said to the Blessed Mother in thanks for something or when you request a favor. As a matter of fact, I think you should write the Hail Mary and the Our Father in your notebook." So, she did.

"Oh, and one more thing," I added. "When you go to Mass, sit, stand, and kneel when everyone else does. And don't worry about

Communion because you won't go up for it. You have the option to sit in your pew when it happens."

Next, we moved on to the basics of Presbyterianism. She told me it was started by a guy named John Calvin in the sixteenth century whose principles stated that God is the biggest authority in the universe. Salvation through Jesus is essential and needs to be shared with the whole world. Unlike the Catholic church, the Presbyterian church is governed at all levels, not just by ministers and religious people, but also by regular people.

"Is your service like a Catholic Mass?" I asked.

"Only in a few ways. You won't ever have to kneel. And you'll stand only to sing hymns, say certain prayers, or recite the Affirmation of Faith and the Doxology. We have Communion in which you dip bread into a cup of wine." I scribbled everything down.

When we were finished talking about religion, Daven asked, "Do you smoke? Because I don't want to do that."

"Yeah, I do every so often. But you don't have to. If anyone asks you why you're not smoking, just tell them you're quitting cold turkey."

"I'm not touching marijuana or illegal drugs, either," she said.

"That's fine, too. Tell everyone you're adopting better habits."

"I can down a beer occasionally to make myself look convincing," she said. "I'm okay with that."

"That's fine."

"Oh, and I know we're supposed to wear each other's clothes, but I think we should stick to our own underwear, makeup, and other personal products."

"That's a good idea," I said. "I didn't even think of that."

"I say we knock off for the day," she said. Our lessons stopped, and I spent the rest of my time there watching MTV and other shows on TV and talking to her about nothing special.

Chapter Seven

Daven

We covered a lot of ground during boot camp, and the next day, Friday, was essentially one of review. We reviewed pictures of family and friends and identified songs and bands once more. I again took Lorraine through fine-dining etiquette and a table setting, this time introducing her to finger bowls. I explained that they were presented just before the dessert course to wash your fingers before leaving the table. She remembered everything she had been taught and took more notes, too.

We were eating lunch when something important popped into my head. We had been so busy with boot camp that I had neglected to tell her sooner. "I – I mean, you—have an invitation to go to a ball in August. It's going to be held at the Stonehurst estate in Villanova. The gown you'll wear is in that little room behind my closet. You can go stag if you don't want to ask for a date; I haven't RSVP'd yet."

Her eyes grew wide. "A ball?"

"Yes, a ball! It's hosted by Oliver and Claire Danford, my parents' friends."

"Wow, just like Cinderella!"

"Yes, just like Cinderella. The RSVP is in the top drawer of my desk. Try to send it in as soon as you can. You can go stag, and it's probably best that you do. Considering the circumstances, you may not want to involve yourself with anyone."

"This is, like, totally awesome!" she said, and I laughed at her enthusiasm.

We played a few more games of tennis and croquet, and I was pleased to see that her technique at both had improved. She also put me through a review of aspects of her life and was satisfied that I had learned at least as much as I would need to get me through a summer of being her. We were so satisfied with each other's progress that we decided to take off from boot camp the following day.

Lorraine

With one more day to go until the switcheroo, I decided to have a last hurrah at Finnegan's Pool, which was at 69th and Grovers in Southwest Philly. Mom and Grandmom came, too. Mom spent the day chatting with her friends, and Grandmom with a bunch of old ladies. She was a trip! She just plunked into a beach chair with her oxygen tank propped up next to her, as if it was just a natural part of her and no bother at all. I took my innertube and bellyflopped with it into the pool. Then I flipped onto my back and let myself drift peacefully. I was wearing a pair of sunglasses that looked just like Alex Van Halen's, so I was looking pretty cool.

"Every Breath You Take" by the Police was playing on a boombox nearby, and I sang along to it out loud, not caring how dumb I looked. I wanted to get as much out of this day at Finnegan's as I could because it could be the last time I'd be able to go there that summer. As I bobbed along, I ran through all the stuff I learned about Daven that week, drilling myself on the names of her family and friends, what they looked like, and all her likes and interests, and how to play croquet and tennis and sit properly at a table. I was really scared about the switcheroo, but I was excited, too. If nothing else, it would get me out of my shitty neighborhood for a summer, and I would be living in a really grand fashion in a Main Line mansion on top of it all.

I felt another innertube bump up against mine and flipped up my shades to see who it was. It was Bobby, bobbing along the same as I was.

"Hey, Kowalski," he said. "Whadaya say about going out?"

"In your dreams, dude," I said and pushed off away from him. Sonofabitch, he followed right after me!

"C'mon, stop playing hard to get! Let's just go out!"

Any other time, I'd have probably said yes. But considering what was about to happen between me and Daven, I couldn't. Hooking up with him would screw everything up, and at a really bad time.

"No, Bobby, just no. I don't wanna."

"Fine. Suit yourself," he said as he pushed off in the opposite direction. I reminded myself to warn Daven about him because, of course, he would probably try again, and on her, thinking she was me. I flipped my shades back down and went back to singing along with the song.

Daven

One day to go until Lorraine and I made the switch. I wanted to enjoy my final day of normalcy, and I did it by sitting on an oversized, comfortable wicker chair in the sunroom with a glass of chardonnay as I flipped through an issue of *Town and Country*. What I was about to do with Lorraine was risky and potentially dangerous, and I needed to take the edge off my frazzled nerves by relaxing with an alcoholic beverage that my parents would have forbidden me. Lord knew the trouble we could get into if we got caught. But it would only be for a short time; we would switch back to our true selves in only two and a half months. No one would ever learn of the identity switch so long as we were careful.

I chose to stay at Arnant alone that summer rather than spend it with my parents at the shore or go on a European tour, as Clay did. I needed time to myself after a whirlwind senior year of high school that had been jam-packed with college interviews, balls, and the myriad social obligations I was required to keep. After eighteen years, my parents had finally shortened my tether and trusted me enough to be on my own.

Also, something in me had told me to stay alone at Arnant, and I understood it now: it must have known that Lorraine and I were going to meet. It sent my parents and my brother away, keeping their prying eyes off my business and giving me the freedom I needed to pull off the identity switch. All the planets had fallen into alignment, so how could I not want to do it?

I drained my glass and retired to my bedroom. Before I fell asleep, I took out my boot-camp notebook and studied all the notes I had taken on Lorraine's life for at least an hour. I could keep my eyes open no more, and I closed the book and slipped into sleep.

Chapter Eight

Lorraine

The big day was finally here. I got up late the next morning and put the stuff I'd need over the next two and a half months into a tote bag. I made sure other things I needed were in my pocketbook, too. Luckily, Mom was at work, and Grandmom was in her room asleep. I told her I was going to be out for most of the day, and she just mumbled something, farted, and rolled back to sleep. I ran out of the house, up to The Avenue, and waited for the next trolley into Center City. It came in a few minutes, so I hopped on it and took it to Fifteenth Street, where I got off and walked across Suburban Station to the R5 train that would take me to Haverford.

I got off at Haverford and walked the mile to Arnant as fast as I could, and I was so nervous the whole time. When I got to the front door, I didn't even have to knock. Daven saw me coming and flung it open. Without saying a word, she took me upstairs to her bedroom and hugged me.

"This is it, Rainey," she said, and she was crying a little. "Thank you so much for doing this for me. I promise to be the best you I can be!"

"And I promise to be the best you I can be," I said, a little teary-eyed myself.

"I know you'll do splendidly! Let's change into each other's clothes." I walked into her bathroom and took off my cutoff T-shirt, cutoff jeans, socks, and sneakers and handed them through the door to her. She then handed me the outfit she was wearing: a pink-and-white seersucker dress that tied at the shoulders with little strings and a pair of espadrilles. I brushed out my hair and put it in a ponytail like hers. She took out her ponytail, brushed out her hair, and used a curling iron to feather it just like mine.

When we were done, we looked at each other and tried not to cry. "I think we look exactly like each other. I don't think anyone could tell us apart," she said. She hugged me again, and I hugged her right back.

"To be clear," she said, "we'll end this identity switch on Saturday, August 20th. On that day, you'll grab your stuff, and I'll grab mine. We'll bring ourselves and our stuff to Suburban Square and do the switcheroo in the bathroom at Strawbridge and Clothier. We'll prearrange an exact meeting time as the day gets closer. I know you don't know where Suburban Square is, but you will by the time that day comes. When we're finished, you'll return to your life, and I'll return to mine."

"Got it! Okay, you know the drill," I told her. "Call me every night from the payphone in front of Titans. Don't call me from my house because it's too risky. Leave a message letting me know you're okay if you don't get a hold of me. If there's a night when you can't call me, I'll understand. Just call me as soon as possible."

"Yes, got it," she said.

"Do you remember how to take public from here to Southwest Philly?" I quizzed her.

"Yes. I go to the Haverford train station and take the train to Suburban Station. Once I'm there, I walk over to the 11 trolley and get off at 67th and The Avenue, and I walk to your house from there," she said.

"Good! Make sure you bring enough money with you for the commute," I told her.

"The gate code. Remember, it's 2628, and the code for the house alarm is 8225," she said.

"Got it," I said.

"Oh, one more thing." She walked over to her pocketbook. "Let's switch pocketbooks. But first, we'll take out little things we'll need, like lip gloss and gum and things like that. And give me your tote bag so I can fill it with my essentials, and I'll leave mine behind."

"Okay," I said as we did the switcheroos. But as I did that, I felt a little guilty that I was abandoning Lorraine Kowalski, abandoning myself. So, along with my lip gloss and a pack of gum, I took out my school ID. Just so I could keep myself close during my time at Arnant.

"Don't worry," I said when I saw Daven give me a worried look. "I won't keep this in your wallet. I'll put it away somewhere where no one will find it."

"Okay," she said. I think the reality of the situation really hit her then because she must have realized why I wanted to hold onto my school ID, and she teared up.

"Well, this is it. You'd better go," I told her. She gave me one more hug before she walked out of her bedroom and on her way into my life.

Daven

I followed Lorraine's instructions exactly for the commute to Southwest Philly. As I walked to the Haverford train station, I didn't think anyone who looked at me could tell I was a Main Line debutante. I'm sure all they saw was the shabbily-dressed burnout girl who was so obviously in the wrong neck of the woods. My legs wobbled when I had first set out from Arnant but strengthened as I continued to the train station. By the time I got there, my breathing had slowed, and I had stopped shaking.

The train to Center City pulled up about twenty minutes later and brought me to Suburban Station in less than half an hour. I followed the signs for the subway-surface trolley line and hopped on the next number eleven trolley that rolled by. That trolley ride moved in a blur, and the next thing I knew, I was hopping off at 67th and Woodland. I walked a block down to Bonnaffon Street, which was a rather rundown collection of row homes, looked for Lorraine's house, and found it.

I climbed the front steps to a porch cluttered with a high stack of old newspapers, a cracked plastic bin filled with tools, two broken chairs, and a small table missing a leg. The front window sported a crack that was taped over with duct tape. I pulled open the rickety storm door; its screen was caked in dust and was dirty, too. Illumination glowed through the small, dirty window in the main door, which was cracked and chipped.

I pushed it open and walked into the sorriest living room I'd ever seen. The walls were light-blue, nicotine-stained, and cracked. Random pictures hung here and there, one of which was Lorraine's senior portrait. The sofa was dark-green and showed many holes and rips. The coffee table that fronted it was piled with magazines, newspapers, several issues of *TV Guide*, a few dirty coffee mugs, and an ashtray filled with cigarette butts. The dark-blue carpeting looked filthy. Dilapidated lamps, one of which had a shade with a huge gash cut into it, glowed dimly from equally dilapidated end tables.

Sitting on opposite ends of the sofa, like bookends, were Grandmom and Mrs. Kowalski. Grandmom's gray hair was short and choppy, as if it had been cut with hedge clippers. She wore thick-framed black glasses, and a cannula in her nose led to the oxygen tank beside her. She wore a blue-gray men's shirt, a pair of purple polyester pants, and dark-blue sneakers. Mrs. K. wore a green T-shirt, frayed bell-bottom jeans, and bedroom slippers. Her dark hair was streaked with gray and hung halfway down her back. She had dark eyes and fine features, and I could tell that she had been beautiful once. She looked haggard and worn-out now, and I got the feeling she wasn't older than her mid-40s. They watched *Action News*, and Grandmom let out a raspy laugh at Jim O'Brien's antics.

"Dinner's done," Mrs. K. barked as soon as I walked in. "It's in the crock pot. We were waiting for you to come home. Where were you?"

I took a deep breath and prayed my feigned Southwest Philly accent wouldn't fail me. "Up at Titans," I said. "I was playing Joust and hangin' out with Bobby and them other guys."

She looked at Lorraine's tote bag, which, of course, was full of my things. I prayed she wouldn't ask to look inside it. "What's in there?" she asked, pointing at it.

"Just some magazines, records, and tapes I was showing everybody."

They both looked quizzically at me, and my heart plunged into my stomach. "You sound kinda different. Do you have a sore throat or something?" Mrs. K. asked.

"No, I feel fine."

She shrugged. "I guess your voice is maturing. All right, let's eat. I'm starving." We moved into the kitchen and seated ourselves at a white Formica table with gold specks. The chairs were padded and covered in dark-yellow vinyl that was cracked and duct-taped together. The set looked very old, from the early 60s. Grandmom and I took our seats as Mrs. K. ladled beef stew from the crock pot and put the bowls in front of us. She poured us glasses of iced tea and served a plate stacked with several slices of white bread. Next to it, she placed a butter dish and a butter knife.

They talked between themselves as I ate in silence. The less I said, the better, so I kept quiet. After dinner, I offered to help with the dishes. Mrs. K. looked surprised but let me do it. I washed them as they returned to the living room and watched *Tic Tac Dough*. After the dishes were done, I told them I was tired and was turning in early.

I climbed the creaky stairs to Lorraine's room at the back of the house. I closed the door, emptied my items from my tote bag into one of her dresser drawers, and got acquainted with the room and its contents. I hadn't felt tired when I told Grandmom and Mrs. K. I was turning in, but now I began to feel so earnest.

I changed into a set of Lorraine's pajamas and went to the bathroom to brush my teeth and get ready for bed. I had brought my own toothbrush, and Lorraine had taken hers. I put my toothbrush in the toothbrush holder when I was finished, hoping neither Grandmom nor Mrs. K. would question the presence of a strange toothbrush in their bathroom. I turned out the bathroom light and shuffled back to the bedroom.

I was about to slide into bed when I heard muffled noises. I looked out the window and saw a boy and a girl embracing in the back alley, but I darted back from the window before they could see me. I crawled into Lorraine's bed, pulled the frayed blanket to my chin, and fell asleep. I had survived my first night in the Kowalski house.

Chapter Nine

Lorraine

After Daven left, I was all alone in that mansion. It was already creeping me out. I decided to stay in her room for the time being because I felt safer there. I walked over to her stereo and turned it on. The song "Wishing" by A Flock of Seagulls came on, and it felt good to have something breaking the silence. I laid down on the bed and stared at the ceiling, really not knowing what to do next. That changed when her phone rang, scaring the hell out of me.

Dear God, I thought, please let me sound like her. Or, at least, not like some kid from Southwest Philly. I picked up the phone.

"Hello?" I said in the tone of voice Daven drilled into me.

"Uh, hello?" said a woman on the other end. "Daven, is that you?"

I assumed this was Pepper, Daven's mom, so I said, "Yes, Mummy, it's me."

"I don't know why you sound different. Anyway, I'm calling to remind you that the staff is returning tomorrow."

"All right. Is there anything I need to do?" I asked. Man, it was hard to talk this way!

"No, everything's a go. Consuelo will let everybody in, so there's nothing you need to do. They'll probably already be in the house as soon as you get up, as they're coming early."

"Okay, then."

"One more thing, darling. I know you enjoy being home alone, but would you consider coming here to spend time with us? We'd love to see you, and it's too quiet around here."

I didn't know what to say, and to be honest, she had me cornered. I should have said yes, but I didn't feel comfortable enough to go down the shore all by myself and spend time with strangers, even if they were supposed to be my parents.

"Mummy, honestly, I like the peace and quiet here. I've had such a busy school year." I tried my best to remember the grammar lessons Daven taught me and really hoped I was talking in the way she would have.

Pepper gave a long sigh. "We miss you so much here, and it's too quiet. But we understand. This past year has been exhausting for you with finishing school, the balls, and the college interviews. Okay, then. You stay at Arnant by yourself. We're still coming home on August 16th, so we'll be there when Clay comes home from Europe. Well, darling, I'll let you go now. Talk to you again soon! Love you!"

I said goodbye and hung up. I wanted to tell Daven all this right away, but I was forced to wait for her check-in call tomorrow night.

I spent the next few hours in Daven's room, listening to the stereo and reading magazines. When I got hungry, I went downstairs and made a bowl of cereal; I was too on edge to eat anything heavier. When I finished, I went back to her room and changed into one of her nightgowns. It was just beginning to get dark, and it was way too early for me to fall asleep, but that's exactly what I did. My first night at Arnant was over.

Daven

As soon as I awoke the next morning, Mrs. K. announced we were going to the pool. Ordinarily, she would be working, as it was a weekday. But she had a sick day she had to use or lose, so it was off to a day at the pool.

We piled into the Kowalskis' dilapidated old Nova and headed off to the community swimming pool at the other end of Southwest Philly, at the James Finnegan Playground. We entered the pool grounds and found a spot to set up our chairs and other gear. Grandmom and Mrs. K. then migrated off to talk to their friends as I grabbed Lorraine's innertube and flopped into the pool.

While lying on my back on the innertube and drifting along, I slid her sunglasses onto my face. It was a bright, beautiful June day, perfect for spending time at the pool. "Faithfully" by Journey played on the public address. Nearby in the pool, a group of kids played Marco Polo while groups of women stood in clusters talking and gossiping. One of the hot topics was Sally Ride, who had embarked on her historic launch into space just a few days earlier. In the shallower end, mothers floated their babies along, getting them used to the water and raising them to someday be proficient swimmers. A boom box played "I'm Still Standing" by Elton John, and I quietly sang along to it as I bobbed among the Southwest Philadelphia waders.

I felt another innertube bump mine and lifted my sunglasses to see a boy my age right next to me, lying in his innertube the same way I was lying in mine. He wore the same sunglasses as mine and a pair of red swim trunks with a white stripe down the side. He had brown hair and was so cute! Right away, I knew this was Bobby, the boy who was ardently pursuing Lorraine.

"Well, Kowalski, I'm hoping you changed your mind," he said, grabbing my innertube to keep me by his side.

I smiled coyly. "I dunno. I'm thinking about it," I replied in what I hoped was a convincing Southwest Philly accent.

"Well, I know how much you like Stevie Nicks. She's coming to The Spectrum next week, and I bought two tickets off of a scalper yesterday. You're coming with me, like it or not." He punctuated this with a big, engaging grin.

He had really put me in a spot, and I had to think how Lorraine would handle this. I gave a careless little laugh and replied, "Damn, Bobby, why'd you have to go and do that? You know Stevie Nicks is my weak spot, don't you? But seriously, I could've bought the tickets on my own."

"Aw, c'mon, Kowalski! Just go out with me! What the fuck, you know I'm hot for you!"

I looked at him as he awaited my answer. Lorraine had often told me of her vain attempts to fob him off, and I could continue with them.

In fact, I should continue with them, considering that I would never be able to see this relationship through, should I assent to it. But he was every bit as persistent as she had warned me, and I was no match for him. Also, I was beguiled by him and didn't understand why Lorraine didn't like him. Not only was he cute, but he also seemed so sweet and earnest. He patiently bobbed along waiting for an answer, so I gave it to him.

"Yeah, okay, I'll go to the Stevie Nicks concert with you. And," I added, holding my breath, "I'll go out with you, too."

He whooped with glee. "All right! This summer's gonna be totally awesome! Okay, be ready next Monday at five. I'll stop by your house with Danny and Nicky and their girlfriends. We're gonna take the Broad Street Line to The Spectrum 'cause no one feels like driving. It's gonna rock!"

He reached out to grab my hand, and my heart flip-flopped. We stayed like that for an hour before we got out of the pool. As we did, he said, "Hey, bring your stuff over to my spot. Danny and Nicky are there, along with some other people. Someone brought a deck of Uno cards, so we're gonna have this kick-ass Uno tournament." I walked over to the Kowalskis' spot, grabbed my towel and tote bag, and explained to Mrs. K. and Grandmom that I would sit with Bobby and the others.

Bobby hardly let go of my hand that day.

Chapter Ten

Daven

We arrived home late that afternoon. Bobby promised to keep me updated on Stevie Nicks. At around seven, I made my way up to the payphone and called my phone at Arnant. Lorraine answered on the second ring.

"Hi!" I said when she answered. "I have big news for you!"

"And I got big news for you, too, but you go first."

She informed me that my parents were arriving home on August 16th, the same day Clay was due home from Europe. I regaled her with my tale of my day at the pool and the new relationship with Bobby. She was aghast!

"Oh my God, you shouldn't have gotten mixed up with him!" she admonished, and I knew she was right. "Yes," I said meekly, "I know. But I'm sorry, I gave in. He's so cute and sincere. I'm surprised you never pursued him."

"Yeah, well, I got a thing about those Southwest Philly guys. They're all losers. Okay, fine, but just be careful!"

I hesitated to tell her what I did next, knowing she'd be disappointed to miss out. "Oh, we're going to the Stevie Nicks concert next week with Danny, Nicky, and their girlfriends."

"Oh, shit! I've been dying to go to that concert! Oh well, there's nothing I can do about it now."

"Yes, I'm sorry. I wish we could go together. Okay, lovey, I'll end it here. You sleep well." We said our goodbyes, and I hung up the phone. Since I was just down the street from Titans, I thought I might as well venture in and check it out.

To say Titans's clientele looked like a rough crowd would be an understatement; they were by far the most nefarious-looking bunch of people I had ever encountered. Instinct told me to play it cool and not bring ire upon myself. This was Lorraine's hangout; bolting out of there wasn't an option. The room was large and dark and full of cigarette smoke. Ambient lighting emanating from the arcade machines illuminated the otherwise dark room, and rough-looking burnout kids clustered around each machine. The Def Leppard song "Photograph" blasted from the jukebox. I wandered through the room, looking for refuge. I found it at a Donkey Kong machine as I took my place among the handful of spectators watching a girl with feathered hair and feather earrings play.

I was so absorbed in the game that I didn't see someone approach me from the side. "Well, Lorraine, what's up? Haven't seen you in a while." I turned to face the most reptilian man I had ever seen, and I knew immediately that this was that slimeball Joe DiGiacomo that Lorraine had warned me about.

"Hey, Joe," I responded in the flattest voice I could muster.

"When's our date? I still have to show you my crib in Springfield."

"Bug off, Joe. You know I'm not interested."

"Ah, so that's how you're gonna be. Playin' hard to get, eh?"

"No, I told you already: I don't want to date you." He was taken aback at that, and frankly, I was slightly frightened. From how Lorraine had spoken of him, he seemed like a dangerous man.

He let out a laugh that sounded more like a hiss. "Well, I'll wait. I'll be here. I ain't goin' nowhere." He curled an arm around me and pulled me close to him. I pushed him away from me and sprinted out the door. I collided with someone as soon as my feet landed on the sidewalk. It was Bobby.

"Yo, easy there! I was gonna call you. But I can tell you now: I'm taking you on a date tomorrow night. We're going to Dennis Pizza down the street. How's six o'clock work for you?"

I forced myself to compose quickly from what had happened with Joe, and I calmly answered, "Six is good."

"All right. I'll come to get you at your house, and we'll walk up to Dennis together." He kissed me on the side of the face before he walked away. I walked away, too, back to the Kowalski house.

Lorraine

I woke up at around eight the next morning. I took a long shower in Daven's bathroom. It was three times the size of my bathroom on Bonnaffon Street that I had to share with Mom and Grandmom. The shower stall was huge and took up one corner of the bathroom. On the other side was a tub that looked like a big pink seashell. There were plants on tall stands and a statue of a woman with no arms. I think Daven said her name was the Venus de Milo.

When I was done, I dried myself off and changed into her clothes. Her walk-in closet was almost the size of my bedroom on Bonnaffon Street. I pulled out a short-sleeved white blouse, a maroon-and-white plaid skirt, and white moccasins and put them on. I styled my hair just like Daven's, with ends that curled under, and wrapped a white ribbon around my head. When I looked in the mirror, no one would ever know by looking at me that I was just some burnout kid from Southwest Philly. I looked just like a rich preppy girl.

I walked down to the kitchen and was startled to see a maid there, even though Pepper already told me about this. She was a Spanish-looking woman and said, "*Buenos días, Señorita Daven,*" to me with a big smile. Daven told me that this meant "good morning," so I smiled back at her and said likewise. This must have been Consuelo, the main housekeeper.

"*¿Te gustaría desayunar?*" I didn't know what that meant, but I assumed she was asking if I wanted breakfast, so I nodded my head. She made scrambled eggs and toast for me and served them with a small bowl of yogurt and a glass of orange juice. I thanked her and ate as fast as I could because there was something I wanted to do that I never got the chance to do until now.

I went back up to Daven's room and walked back into the walk-in closet. There was a door at the back of the closet that led into another, smaller closet. This was where Daven said she kept her gowns. She had a lot of them in there. I saw the one she wore to the deb ball and the one she wore to her graduation. Off to the side was something covered with a white sheet. I pulled the sheet off of it and let out a huge gasp!

It was a gown on a dress form, and it was the most gorgeous gown I'd ever seen! My senior-prom gown was really pretty but looked like a nightgown compared to this one. The gown was midnight-blue satin. It had a ruffled neckline and puffy, off-the-shoulder sleeves that had ruffles, too. The skirt was very full and had a ruffled hemline. When I lifted the skirt, I saw layers of black crinoline dotted everywhere with tiny sequins, like diamonds. Next to it, leaning up against the wall, was a hoop to wear under the skirt. Draped over the hoop, in a clear plastic bag, were a pair of opera-length white gloves. I couldn't believe this was what I was going to wear to the ball! I would be just like Cinderella!

I closed the door of the gown room and walked out of the closet and back into the bedroom. I sat on the sofa and read some *Seventeen* magazines that were on top of the coffee table. I guess I was reading for about an hour when the phone rang, and I jumped. Oh God, I hated talking on the phone! I said a prayer and answered it, trying to sound as much like Daven as I could.

"Hello?" I spoke into the phone, hoping to God my Main Line accent would be realistic.

"Umm, hello, Daven?" squeaked a girl's voice on the line. Of course, I had no idea who it was, so I took a stab in the dark and hoped for the best.

"Bex? Is that you?" I just assumed it was Bex. I thought Bex would be the most likely to call, as she was pretty good friends with Daven.

"Of course, it's me, ssssilly!" She dragged out that S, like the hiss of a snake, and I was relieved that I guessed right. Then, she let out a high-pitched giggle.

"What's going on?"

"Well, Jensen and you and I are going to the cricket match at Haverford College on Saturday," she said.

"Oh, fun! What time should I be ready?"

"The game starts at noon. We'll come for you at eleven."

"Okay, sounds good. See you then!" I hung up fast, not wanting to talk any more than I had to. A cricket match on Saturday; that was three days away. I walked back into the closet to look for something to wear. Something told me it was going to be an important day, and I wanted to look the part.

Daven

True to his word, Bobby came by the house at six the next night. I waited for him, wearing a sleeveless black shirt, cutoff shorts, bunched white sweatsocks, and sneakers. My hair was feathered like Lorraine's, and I wore a pair of her feather earrings. A wide-handled comb in my back pocket completed the look. I took a bottle of Kissing Potion out of my front pocket and slathered it liberally on my lips.

He wore a sleeveless Judas Priest T-shirt, jeans, and high-topped Nike sneakers. A wide-handled comb of his own poked out of his back pocket, and he pulled it out and ran it through his feathered hair. The gold stud earring in his left ear glinted in the sunlight.

He took hold of my hand, and we walked up to The Avenue. When we arrived at Dennis Pizza, he sat me at a booth and walked to the jukebox. He dropped a quarter in the slot and punched in the number of a song. He sauntered up to the counter as "Gimme All Your Lovin'" by ZZ Top blasted out, and he ordered our food.

I observed the people entering and exiting the pizza shop. Many were the neighborhood kids; a few were adults with their young children. I loved being among these Southwest Philly people and watching them. They were so different from the people who had surrounded me all my life.

Our pizza was ready about twenty minutes later. We ate it as we washed it down with Frank's black cherry Wishniak soda. I'd never had that soda before, and I loved the intense cherry flavor.

"Are you excited about seeing Stevie Nicks? The concert's next Monday," he said between bites of pizza.

"Yeah!" I responded. "I was so bummed when I couldn't get tickets for it."

A sly smile. "A friend of mine's a scalper, and he scored tickets for all of us. Like I said at the pool, Danny, Nicky, and their girlfriends are coming with us. It'll be six of us. And we're taking the Broad Street Line to get there."

"I can't wait."

He slid a quarter to me, and I rose and walked to the jukebox. I punched in the number for the song "Mexican Radio" by Wall of Voodoo and returned to the booth.

"I've been wanting to date you for a long time," he said as he stared intensely at me over his soda can.

I had to think fast about an appropriate response Lorraine would say. "Yeah, sorry. I think Southwest Philly guys are losers." I instantly recalled what she had told me during the previous night's conversation.

He smirked, and I appeased him with, "But you won me over." This seemed to please him, for he smiled and grabbed my hand under the table. "I'm serious about you," he said. "I totally dig you. You're different from the other girls around here. Special."

"Special?"

"Yeah, special. Don't forget that."

After we had finished our pizza, we left the pizza shop and walked several blocks to a park on Grays Avenue. He pushed me on the swing for a while, then we sat on a bench and talked. It was almost nine o'clock and starting to get dark, so he walked me back to the Kowalski house. We had our first kiss! It was wonderful!

I thanked him for a good night, and he said he'd call me. I was about to walk into the house when I realized I needed to check in with Lorraine! I waited for Bobby to walk to his home on 67th Street, which was behind Bonnaffon Street. Then, I proceeded to the payphone on The Avenue and dialed my phone number.

"Hey, sorry," I said to Lorraine when she answered. "My date with Bobby ran late."

"It's okay," she said. "If you can't check in at seven because you've been held up, that's okay. How was the date?"

"Excellent. We went to Dennis Pizza as planned. Then we went to the park on Grays Avenue afterward, and he kissed me at your door!" We chatted for a bit longer before bidding each other goodnight and hanging up. Back to the Kowalski house I went.

Chapter Eleven

Lorraine

I was ready at eleven that Saturday morning like Bex told me to be, and I stood on the portico – a portico, not a front porch, Daven told me—waiting for her and Jensen. The outfit I decided on was a mint-green polo shirt, white shorts, white ankle socks, and white Keds. A mint-green ribbon was tied around my hair, and for jewelry, I wore Daven's pearl stud earrings and her Swatch watch. I also carried her Bermuda bag, which was a small pocketbook that had her initials on it. And I wore her Ray-Ban sunglasses, too.

It was just before eleven when a gray Volvo pulled up with two girls seated in the front seat. From Daven's pictures, I knew they were Bex and Jensen, with Bex behind the wheel. They both waved. I climbed into the back seat, and we took off.

They were two typical preppy girls dressed a lot like I was. Bex talked more than Jensen did. They were both giggly and silly and talked non-stop about stuff that happened at The Baldwin School that year. I nodded and giggled along with them, doing my best all the while to talk the way Daven told me to as I commented on the things they said.

Haverford College was less than ten minutes away from Arnant. When we got there, we parked and walked down the road to the cricket field. At the field, I saw a bunch of guys and girls, all dressed like preppies. One guy stood out from the crowd, and I almost dropped dead when I saw him. He was a cross between Richard Gere and Pierce Brosnan and was probably the most beautiful human being I ever laid eyes on. I felt my heart drop right into my stomach. Then I saw him make eye contact with me and head my way, and I thought I was going to throw up.

He looked to be Paulie's age, so like twenty-one or so. He wore a light-blue polo shirt with a white sweater tied around his neck, khaki pants, and docksiders with pale-blue argyle socks. His dark hair was parted on the side and slicked down so it wouldn't move. He kept right on walking toward me, and my legs started to get wobbly.

"Daven Barrett!" he said with a big smile when he came up to me. "Do you remember me from the Charity Ball? Stuart Worthington. I was on the Young Men's Committee."

"Of course!" I lied, real fast.

"Fancy seeing you here! Do you like cricket?"

"It's okay. My friends Bex and Jensen wanted to come, so here I am."

He looked toward them and smiled. "Good day, ladies. I'm Stuart Worthington from Radnor." They introduced themselves back at him.

He took me by the arm and walked us toward the bleachers, and I wanted to faint right then and there. I'm telling you, he was a total fox! "The game's going to start soon; let's get our seats." I looked back at Bex and Jensen, and they covered their mouths to hide their giggles. He found seats for us on the top bleacher, and we sat down. Bex and Jensen sat next to us. Stuart kept his arm wrapped around mine.

Soon, one member from each team came out onto the field, and everyone got quiet. They tossed a coin, and everyone cheered as the players took their positions. It was a big oval field with a rectangle of dirt in the middle. On either end of the dirt rectangle were three wooden posts that Stuart said were called wickets. Nine players arranged themselves on the field, and two at either end of the dirt rectangle. The two on the rectangle held long, wide, curved bats, like big taffies.

A guy came running in from the infield and windmill threw a red baseball at one of the batters. The ball hit the rectangle, popped up, and the batter hit it. The ball flew into the outfield as both batters ran back and forth along the rectangle, and everybody cheered, including Stuart.

It was hard to keep track of everything because so much was going on. It was like baseball, but busier. I tried to follow it but got so confused. "Look how he bowls that ball!" Stuart said when the pitcher, who Stuart called the bowler, struck a guy out. As soon as the guy struck out, some guys from the other team, who were standing behind him, caught the ball, and everyone cheered again.

The game dragged on, and I was clueless as to what was happening. I'd never heard of this sport in my life, and I didn't understand it. At one point, the bowler threw a ball at the wicket, and there was more cheering. "That's it! There goes that bail!" Stuart shouted.

Bex and Jensen kept giggling at us. At one point, Jensen gave me an "okay" sign when Stuart wasn't looking. I tried not to laugh.

The game lasted for about three hours, and I was glad when it was over, because I didn't understand very much of it. We climbed down from the bleachers, and I was about to ask Bex and Jensen what we were going to do next when Stuart said, "Do you ladies mind if I abscond with your friend?"

They giggled. "No, she's all yours, and we'll leave you two lovebirds alone." They said goodbye and that they'd call me soon before they got into the Volvo and drove away.

As the spectators trickled away from the cricket field, Stuart said, "Come, let's go for a walk. The duck pond is just down the road." We walked down the road, still arm in arm, until we got to the duck pond. In it were ducks, geese, and other water birds I never saw before.

"It's wonderful that we can talk like this, now that we finally have a moment to ourselves," he said as he leaned his arms on the split-rail fence that surrounded the duck pond. "I'd have chatted you up more at the Charity Ball, but I was so damned busy on that committee."

"That's all right," I said. "It was a busy night for me, too."

We stared at the birds for a while. It was a really pretty day, and we talked about my life – or, I should say, Daven's life, and I really didn't want it to end. This guy was such a fox, too. I couldn't wait to tell Daven about him. We spent an hour or so making small talk talking about my life – or, I should say, Daven's life, and his, too. He told me he had an older sister named Eunice and two younger sisters named Mamie and Doris. He lived on an estate called Llanwyn in Radnor. His family made its fortune in the Pennsylvania Railroad, the same as Daven's. He went to a school in Malvern called The Phelps School for high school and Princeton University for college. He was going into his senior year at Princeton.

"I want to ask you for a date," he said. "We'll be cazh and go to Gullifty's. How does that work for you? Let's say lunch tomorrow?"

"That would be wonderful," I said.

"I think that's enough bird-watching for one day," he said as he took my hand and guided me away. "I'll take you home now." We walked back to where his Jaguar was parked near the cricket field, got in, and sped off to Arnant.

"Remember, I'll pick you up at noon tomorrow," he said when we pulled up to the portico. Before I got out of the car, he gave me a little kiss on the cheek, and I thought I would melt. I waved as I watched him drive away. I couldn't wait for Daven's call that night.

It came exactly at seven. "Hey," I said, "I met a guy today at the cricket match. His name's Stuart Worthington. You met him at the Charity Ball. He was on the Young Men's Committee."

"Ah, yes, Stuart!" she said. "Isn't he dreamy? He seemed to like me, and I think he wanted to get together, but I couldn't tell. We were both so busy at the Charity Ball that we couldn't talk much. He lives on an estate in Radnor called Llanwyd. He has three sisters: Eunice, Mamie, and Doris. His family also made its fortune in the Pennsylvania Railroad."

"Yeah, he told me all that. He's a total fox," I said. "We're doing lunch at Gullifty's tomorrow. Where is that?"

"On Lancaster Avenue in Bryn Mawr. It's a cute, casual place. You'll like it."

"Okay, that's cool. Anything new on your end?"

"No, I just spent a few hours playing arcade games at Titan's and the rest of the day at home listening to your Van Halen records. I'm getting good at Joust! I have to get one of those machines for the house!"

We both laughed, said our goodbyes, and hung up. Even though it was early, I put on a pair of pajamas and strolled down to the kitchen to make a cup of tea. I was really jittery about tomorrow.

Chapter Twelve

Daven

    I awoke at eight the next morning and shuffled to the kitchen for breakfast. Mrs. K. was already there making a pan of scrambled eggs. "We're going to the ten o'clock mass," she announced, which sent me into a little panic. I hoped I would remember the mass protocol Lorraine had drilled me on during boot camp now that the real thing was coming.

    "Be careful of how you dress," Grandmom told me. I hadn't seen her sitting at the kitchen table until she spoke. "None of those shitty concert shirts you always wear. Try to dress like a lady. And don't forget to bring your rosary and missalette."

    I ate breakfast and hurried upstairs to shower. Afterward, I frantically pawed through Lorraine's closet for something suitable to wear, but I was coming up short. I found a frilly white dress, probably the one she had worn to her graduation, but it seemed too formal. I looked again and saw a light-blue shirt dress with cap sleeves and a black belt, a cheaply-made affair that had "Kmart" written all over it, but it was the best I could do. I pulled it out along with a pair of black flats. This would have to be my mass outfit.

    With my ensemble in order, I scrambled to find the items Grandmom had told me to bring to mass. I knew what a rosary was, but what was a missalette? Lorraine hadn't explained that to me. I looked through all her drawers and found the rosary in the top drawer of her nightstand, along with a small white book detailing the mass's order. This must have been the missalette.

    After I had finished getting ready, I joined Mrs. K. and Grandmom downstairs, and we proceeded directly to St. Clement's Church. It was a long walk, about five blocks, and I reminded myself to follow suit in everything they did inside that church – except for Holy Communion, which, I reminded myself, Lorraine told me I could sit out, as not everyone went up for it.

As soon as we entered, we dipped our hands into a large marble bowl on a pedestal that was situated at the end of the altar and made the sign of the cross. *Forehead, chest, left shoulder, right shoulder. Use your right hand only,* Lorraine's words echoed in my head as I tapped these areas of my body with my fingers. We filed into one of the pews but didn't sit down, and we knelt as we twined our rosaries around our hands. I had never done these things at church; they generated odd feelings in me.

Soon a procession that included the priest made its way up to the altar while a hymn was sung, and we, along with the congregation, stood. Mrs. K., Grandmom, and I opened our missalettes so we could follow the mass. There was a multitude of imagery in this church: statues, a huge crucifix above the altar, depictions of saints in the stained-glass windows, and plaques depicting scenes from Christ's march to his crucifixion—the Stations of the Cross, Lorraine had told me. My church, Bryn Mawr Presbyterian, had none of that. My grandmother complained that Catholics were idolaters; I could see now what she was referring to. Frankly, I liked all the imagery. I liked seeing what these Catholics focused on as they prayed.

Presbyterian Holy Communion is passed in large silver pans to congregation members sitting in their pews. Here, everyone stood up and filed into the center aisle to personally receive Holy Communion from the priest. Mindful of Lorraine's directive, I stayed put as Mrs. K. and Grandmom moved to the center aisle.

After mass, I heaved a sigh of relief for getting through it successfully. I don't think anyone, even Mrs. K. and Grandmom, could tell that I was faking being a Catholic. When we got back to the house, I changed into a T-shirt and a pair of shorts, grabbed one of Lorraine's pimple balls, and went out to the backyard. It was all cement without a blade of grass showing anywhere. As I played with the ball, I wondered what Lorraine was doing at that moment and hoped her date with Stuart would go well.

Lorraine

Just like he said he would, Stuart got to Arnant at noon. I was waiting for him on the portico. I hoped my outfit would be good for the occasion: I wore a sleeveless white blouse, a long khaki skirt, and espadrilles, and I carried the Bermuda bag again. I hopped in his Jaguar, and off we went to Gullifty's.

It was very close, about ten minutes from Arnant. Daven was right: it was a cute little place, and I liked it. I liked the way it was decorated with mirrors and wooden hutches along the walls. A waitress came to take our drinks as soon as we were seated. Stuart ordered a club soda, and I got a Coke. The waitress came back with our drinks a few minutes later, and we were ready to order. He got the roast-beef sandwich, and I got a tuna salad on rye.

After the waitress left, he grabbed my hands under the table, and my heart flip-flopped. "Thank you for coming out today. This means a lot to me."

"Same here."

"I foresee many great things in your future," he said with a big smile.

"Oh, really? Like what?"

"Hmm, let's see. I see a polo match, dinner at Le Bec-Fin, and perhaps mixed doubles at the Merion Cricket Club with one of my sisters and her husband."

That was a lot to take in! I didn't know what Le Bec-Fin was, but I assumed it was a restaurant if we were going to have dinner there. "That sounds divine," I said, imitating Daven as best I could.

"And I couldn't be more pleased to do all those things with you," he said, looking deep into my eyes. My heart flipped-flopped again.

Our sandwiches came, and as we ate them, I suddenly remembered what I needed to ask him. "Oh, I'm going to a ball in August at the

Stonehurst estate in Villanova. Saturday the sixth, to be exact. Would you like to come with me?"

"I'd adore it! I know Stonehurst well. What time does it start?"

"Eight o'clock."

"I'll arrive in a limo at seven. We'll have a dashing time!"

I was glad to have gotten that out of the way! I didn't want to go stag to that ball. We finished lunch, and then he took me back to Arnant.

"Next time, I'll bring you to Llanwyn," he told me before I got out of his car. "I think you'll find it smashing. And with luck, you can meet my family."

He kissed me on the cheek. I climbed out and waved goodbye as he rolled down the driveway and out onto the road. I ran up to Daven's room, found the Stonehurst invitation, and filled out the RSVP. I changed into one of her rompers and her Keds and tucked the RSVP into my pocket. I found her bike in the shed at the end of the estate, and I hopped on it and rode up to the Haverford Post Office, where I mailed the RSVP.

It was such a nice day that I didn't see a reason to rush back to Arnant, so I took a little ride through that part of the Main Line. It really hit me that though I was only a few miles away from Southwest Philly, I actually felt as if I was a million miles away from it. I rode up to Haverford College and saw the duck pond, where I talked with Stuart after the cricket match. Then I crossed over Lancaster Avenue and up to Montgomery Avenue and saw the Merion Cricket Club, the country club Daven belonged to where Stuart said we'd play doubles. I kept pedaling and passed Bryn Mawr College, Rosemont College, and then Villanova University. Villanova's chapel sat right on Lancaster Avenue, and it was a beautiful one with two steeples soaring into the air. I wished I could have gone to mass there! Daven told me Stonehurst was close to Villanova, but I couldn't find it. I assumed Stuart would know where it was.

I turned around when I hit Villanova and rode through the back roads of Bryn Mawr and Haverford on my way back to Arnant. There was one beautiful mansion after another, and I was sorry Mom and Grandmom weren't with me so that I could show them.

I got back to Arnant a few hours later. I was hungry again, so Consuelo, the maid, served me dinner of turkey, mashed potatoes, and corn, which I gobbled up. Daven's call was going to ring in soon, so I went back to her room right after dinner so I'd be ready for it.

It came a little after seven. "What's up?" I asked.

"I survived Mass!" she said, and she sounded happy. "I've been playing pimple ball for most of the day. I didn't know how much fun those little balls were!"

I gave her a quick rundown of my date with Stuart. When I asked her what Le Bec-Fin was, she gasped. "That's a restaurant in town. It's the best in Philly, and I think even in the whole country! Lucky you! My parents took me there for dinner the night of my graduation! You'll love it!"

"Stuart is a pretty awesome dude," I said.

"He certainly sounds like it!"

I told her that Stuart said he'd go with me to the Stonehurst ball, and she was happy that I found a date.

"Oh," she said, "I'm going to the Stevie Nicks concert with Bobby, Nicky, and Danny tomorrow night, so I may not get home till late. I probably won't be able to call you, as I don't want to have to walk up to The Avenue to use the payphone at that time of night." I told her that was fine and that she could do her check-in call the next night. I was really bugged that I was missing out on that concert, but there was nothing I could do about it.

We chatted a little more and then said our goodbyes. At eight o'clock, I turned on Daven's TV and watched *Archie Bunker's Place*. I couldn't wait to see what my next date with Stuart would bring.

Chapter Thirteen

Daven

Bobby, Danny, and Nicky arrived at the house at six the next night. Danny and Nicky were accompanied by their girlfriends, Lynn McBride and Carol Taylor.

"Let's buy some lighters," Bobby said as soon as I walked out the door. The gang of us promptly made our way to a store called the Paschall Variety at the corner of 66th Street and Paschall Avenue, about two blocks from Lorraine's house. A dark-haired teenage boy wearing a blue West Catholic T-shirt stood behind the counter, and he sold us a six-pack of Bic lighters. "The Safety Dance" by Men Without Hats played from the boombox on a shelf behind him.

I had no idea why we needed Bic lighters and was afraid to ask, for Lorraine would know why. Nicky unknowingly enlightened me, saying, "Everyone hold these up high as soon as Stevie takes the stage!" Bobby distributed the lighters all around, and I put mine in the cross-body handbag I carried. We were all thirsty, so we bought sodas, too.

We trooped up to The Avenue and hopped on the next 11 trolley that rolled by. It took us to the 15th Street Station in about half an hour. From there, we took the Broad Street Line to complete the remainder of the journey to The Spectrum.

The train to the Spectrum was a happy, noisy place, full of kids and young adults chattering excitedly about the impending concert. A guy walked up and down the aisle, hawking Stevie Nicks concert shirts, and a scalper hawked tickets.

"Hey, buddy!" Bobby yelled over to the concert-shirt guy. "Gimme one right here!" Money and a concert shirt switched hands, and the next thing I knew, the concert shirt was sitting on my lap!

"Bobby!" I cried. "You didn't have to do that!"

"Yes, I did!" He pulled me closer to him and kissed me on the mouth. I was touched by the simple gesture of him buying me a shirt. Danny and Nicky followed suit and bought shirts for Lynn and Carol.

I folded the shirt into a small square and stuffed it into my bag. Of course, it would be for Lorraine, and I was certain she would love this souvenir.

We disembarked at the end of the line at Pattison station and walked up Broad Street to The Spectrum. We arrived to find hordes of people waiting to be admitted into the venue, and scalpers were everywhere attempting to drum up last-minute ticket sales. We took our places in line, and soon, the doors opened. Everyone was frisked before entry because, Bobby explained, they didn't want anyone bringing in cameras or recording devices. I was hesitant about this, but a lady, not a man, frisked me by giving me a quick pat-down and peeking inside my bag. We were then cleared for entry, and we ran into the arena.

We bought tour books, and I stuffed mine into my bag, again another souvenir for Lorraine.

Our seats were to the left of the stage. They weren't close to it but weren't nosebleeds, either. Workers were setting up equipment and musical instruments. Then the lights went down, and I thought Stevie Nicks would take the stage. But a man came out instead, and everyone cheered. His name was Joe Walsh, and I knew this because Bobby shouted out his name as soon as Joe Walsh took the stage. I assumed he was a famous musician. He sang a beautiful song called "Sentimental Lady," and the crowd went wild. Best of all, Bobby held his arm around me and sang the whole thing to me.

The lights were extinguished after Joe Walsh finished his performance and left the stage. Immediately we flicked our lighters and held them aloft, as did the crowd, and the entire stadium was cast aglow. I had never seen anything like it. Stevie Nicks entered the stage dressed in a sequined white gown, and the crowd went wild. She approached the microphone and began to sing a song called "Gold Dust Woman," which I knew from Lorraine was a Fleetwood Mac song that Stevie had sung the lead vocals for.

I was familiar with Stevie's canon only because of Lorraine, but she didn't have one bad or mediocre song. Every song she sang had me cheering and yelling for more! One particularly memorable song, "Beauty and the Beast," almost reduced me to tears. She was a gifted performer, and I was sorry when the show ended.

As we exited the arena, Nicky asked, "Are youse hungry? Because we can go up to the Oregon Diner if youse want. It's kind of a walk, but I'm up for it if youse are." We agreed that we could all use something to eat, so we began the hike up Broad Street to Oregon Avenue and the diner.

I ordered a tossed salad and a small bowl of Jello, both of which I scarfed down. We were still excited about the concert and discussed it non-stop as we ate. After our meal, we hiked down Oregon Avenue to the Oregon station and returned to Southwest Philly.

Bobby walked me to the door and kissed me goodnight. I thanked him for the lovely night out, and he said he would call me the next day. It was past one a.m. I unlocked the door and let myself into the house. Mrs. K. and Grandmom were both asleep. I quietly climbed the stairs to Lorraine's room, put the tour book and the shirt in one of her dresser drawers, and got ready for bed. I fell asleep to strains of "Beauty and the Beast" drifting through my head.

PART TWO

July 1983

Chapter Fourteen

Lorraine

I went to Llanwyn on the first Saturday of July. I knew this was going to be a big deal, so I wore one of Daven's Lilly Pulitzer dresses and a pair of white sandals. And I carried the Bermuda bag yet again. Llanwyn was fifteen minutes away in Radnor, so we got there pretty fast.

Llanwyn was at the end of this long, curving driveway. It was a two-story brick mansion with two wings that jutted out of the front of it and a roof with six chimneys! I had never seen a house with six chimneys! We pulled up to the huge wooden front door and were greeted by a butler! It was just like you see in the movies!

"Good afternoon, Mr. Worthington," he said.

"Good afternoon, Ronald. May I present Miss Daven Barrett?" I smiled, and Ronald gave a quick nod of his head and led us into the mansion. It was as fancy as Daven's. Ronald led us into a room with four armchairs situated in a circle in front of a fireplace. In the middle of the chairs was a low, oval-shaped table. Right above the fireplace was a painting of a woman, maybe Stuart's grandmother, judging by how old the painting looked.

"Stuart!" said a woman who was entering the room with a man right behind her as Ronald departed. These must have been Stuart's parents, and they were.

"Daven, I'd like to introduce you to my parents, Mildred and George Worthington. Mummy and Daddy, this is Daven Barrett." They happily shook my hand and told me they were delighted to meet me. Mildred told me to call her Milly. They looked a lot like Daven's parents, judging by what I saw in Daven's photo albums. They were very rich- and preppy-looking. We sat in the armchairs, and in a few minutes, a maid brought us lunch on a silver platter.

"I hope you like watercress sandwiches," Milly said as she put the sandwiches on plates and passed them around to us. I bit into one and was surprised because I never had a sandwich with cream cheese and radishes before.

While we were eating, Stuart said, "I have exciting news. Daven and I are attending the Stonehurst ball next month."

"That's wonderful!" Milly said. "Claire Danford and I were classmates at Barnard. She and Oliver are wonderful people; you'll love them!"

After we finished lunch, George, said, "How about a game of croquet? Are you two up for it?"

Stuart answered for both of us. "Of course!" he said. We all got up and walked through some other rooms in the mansion and out to the backyard. That backyard stretched for miles, it seemed. I never saw so much green in one place. I think it was even bigger than Daven's backyard. The croquet field had already been set up for us. I flashed back to my croquet lessons during boot camp and hoped I would be able to play a good game.

We picked out our balls; I got the blue one. Red was the top color on the stake, so Stuart went first. He hit his ball with his mallet, and it passed through the wicket. He moved on to the next wicket, and his ball passed through that one, too. On the next wicket, his ball didn't go through, so now it was my turn.

I took a deep breath and said a prayer as my mallet struck my ball. The ball passed through the wicket, and I was relieved. I moved onto the next one, and the next. All my practice with Daven had paid off!

We worked our way through the croquet course, and George even knocked my ball out of the boundary with his! He really wanted to earn that bonus stroke and finish first! As it turned out, Milly finished first, beating us all.

When the game was over, we went back inside for drinks. Everyone but me drank old-fashioneds; I had a soda. I wanted an old-fashioned, but no one wanted me to drink on account of being underage. About an hour later, Stuart announced he was taking me home. I told his parents nice to meet you, and goodbye, and we went back to Arnant.

"Next time, let's play doubles at Merion with my sister Eunice and her husband Cullen," he said as he pulled up to the front door. "They live in Bar Harbor and are coming down in a few weeks. I'll keep you posted." I got a little queasy hearing this because I wasn't all that great of a tennis player, even though I played a lot of tennis during boot camp.

"I'm a little rusty," I said. "I haven't played in a while."

"Don't fear, we'll get you back into the swing of things!" he said with a laugh and a swinging motion of his arm. He kissed me on the cheek, and I told him I'd keep in touch before I jumped out of the car and walked into the house.

When Daven called that night, I told her about the upcoming tennis game at the Merion Cricket Club. "Don't forget to wear all white," she said. "They have a strict dress code. Everything has to be white. My tennis clothes are near the back of my closet along with my tennis racket. And my membership card is in the top drawer of my desk."

"I'm so nervous," I told her. "I didn't do all that good when you taught me tennis during boot camp."

"You'll be fine," she said. "Tell them you haven't played in a while if they ask questions."

She ended the conversation by telling me that her and Bobby were spending a lot of time at Titans playing Joust and Pole Position, and they were spending a lot of time at his house playing Atari, too. We said goodnight. I walked over to her stereo and tuned it to 94 WYSP. "Say What You Will" by Fastway blasted out, and I started banging my head to it. Of course, I turned it down to a low volume in case any of the servants were close enough to hear it. Even though I was all alone in

Daven's bedroom, and her family wasn't around, I still worked hard to keep up the charade.

Chapter Fifteen

Daven

During the second week of July, a marvelous thing happened: Bobby bought his first car, a tan, 1970 Dart, a muscle car, he proudly informed me. He dangled a Playboy air freshener from the rear-view mirror; I suppose he thought it looked cool. He bought the car with the money he had earned unloading the delivery trucks at Moore's, a furniture store on The Avenue.

On the day he bought the Dart, we were hanging out on the corner of Paschall and Bonnaffon, with the Dart parked in the street next to us. We happily chugged Budweiser while listening to "White Wedding" by Billy Idol, celebrating Bobby's new purchase. Danny, Nicky, Lynn, and Carol were with us, too.

"Hey," Danny piped up between sips of Budweiser, "I was in Titans yesterday and saw that Joe just got Mario Brothers, that new arcade game everyone's been talking about. Whadaya say we go up there and play it?" We agreed. Nicky, who owned the boom box, turned it off and took it back to his house, a short distance from the street. When he returned, we finished our beer, stacked the empty cans on the curb, and set out for Titans, excited to play the new game.

We entered to find the usual scene with throngs of kids surrounding the arcade machines and the air thick with omnipresent cigarette smoke. "Burning Heart" by Vandenberg blasted from the jukebox. The beer I had just drunk churned in my stomach. I wasn't keen on beer but had to drink it because Lorraine did. I hoped I wouldn't throw it back up. Mario Brothers was occupied, so we killed time playing Q-Bert. After half an hour or so, Mario Brothers became available, and we raced to it before someone else did.

Bobby dropped a quarter in the machine, and it played a happy tune as a little man in blue overalls appeared. He ran along several platforms and jumped to knock turtles, called Koopa Troopas, off the platforms to earn points. He gained more points by catching the coins that dropped from the top of the platforms. Bobby was doing great! We all cheered! Other kids gathered around us to cheer him on, too.

I turned away from the arcade game to go to the back of the building to use the bathroom. As I was leaving, a hand clamped around my arm. I looked up into Joe DiGiacomo's sinister face, and my heart plummeted.

"You're not gonna give it up easy, are you, Lorraine?" he sneered.

"Joe, lemme go!" I cried.

He dragged me into the office, where a sinister-looking guy in his early twenties was seated at the desk. I had no idea who he was or what his function was, either.

"Keep your eye on her," Joe barked at him. I dared not move as Joe grabbed a pen and a piece of paper from the desk and scrawled the words, *"Holstein in an hour. Be there or lose Lorraine!"* on it. He handed it to the guy, who took it with a sinister grin.

"Give that to Bobby Murphy in ten minutes," he ordered. "And you and the crew come to Holstein, too, right after you do that. Kick everyone out before you go and lock the place up." He hustled me out the back door of the building and to his Trans Am, which was parked in the back alley. He flung open the passenger door, pushed me into the seat, and jumped in on the driver's side before starting the car and throwing it into gear. We sped down the alley onto a side street and then banked a sharp right turn onto The Avenue.

"Where are you taking me?" I croaked in terror, as Southwest Philly flew past us.

"Don't worry about it. You'll see when you get there," he snapped. I recalled the note he had written; the word *Holstein* was on it. Were we going to this Holstein place? What kind of place was it? Was I going to be murdered there? Joe looked like the kind of guy who would have had no qualms about committing a homicide. I trembled at this thought.

We turned left onto 70th Street and drove for many blocks. We passed row homes and corner stores and drove past a huge brick school building. We crossed the intersection at Lindbergh Boulevard, and soon after, we passed over a bridge and entered an industrial corridor with buildings all around us. We turned at a car dealership, and a glance at the street sign above me told me we were on Holstein Avenue. Holstein was a street! But what significance did it hold for Joe, and why had he commanded Bobby to meet him there?

We pulled into a nearby parking lot, and he shut off the engine; it had begun to grow dark. "Why are you doing this?" I asked. Although I should have been thinking about a million more important things, a work of art I was required to study in preparation for my art history major at Vassar flashed through my mind: *Abduction of a Sabine Woman* by the sixteenth-century sculptor Giambologna. It depicted a man carrying off a woman from another man, who can only helplessly watch the horror unfold. The three figures represented to me Bobby, Joe, and me. How insane it was that I should have thought of art at a time like this!

"Because I've been wanting you for a long time. Now that you're legal, we can be together."

I was dumbfounded, and he continued. "Look, Lorraine, you're different from the other girls at Titan's. I can tell you're not loose. You're the best wife material I know."

"You want to marry me?" I croaked.

"Yeah, I sure as hell do. To be honest, I wish I could carry you off to a Justice of the Peace right now and get it done. Wife you up fast."

I swallowed the sour taste that rose in my throat. "But I don't love you, Joe. I just don't. I wanna go back to Titan's, so please take me back there now."

"Why? So you can fly back into the arms of Bobby What's-His-Face? Ah, screw that little punk! You need a real man." He leaned closer, and his cheap cologne filled my nostrils. His shirt was unbuttoned halfway down his chest, displaying a mat of dark hair, and tangled within it was a gold, oval-shaped medallion on a gold chain. The medallion bore an image of the Blessed Mother. Although I was merely passing myself off as Lorraine – and, by extension, also as a Catholic – I nevertheless prayed to the Blessed Mother in earnest, beseeching her to forgive my Protestant ways and begging for her help.

He reached up to stroke my face; I pulled back in disgust. He laughed softly. "You're gonna be that way, eh? That's fine. Because soon Bobby'll be here with his crew. Mine's coming, too. Me and Bobby are gonna have a race. The winner gets you, but nobody beats me, ever. I always win no matter what I have to do to make it happen. You're gonna be mine by the end of the night even on the slim chance that I lose. When the race is over, I'll take you to your new home. Tomorrow, we'll shop for wedding rings."

This was the most revolting thing anyone had ever said to me. Was he serious? Were he and Bobby really going to have this duel, with the prize being me? Was Joe really planning on carrying me off as his soon-to-be bride? My God, what kind of world was this? It was an utterly barbaric one, that's what kind it was!

He clamped his hand to the back of my head, and I couldn't break away. I gagged as he jammed his tongue into my mouth. He unbuttoned his shirt the rest of the way as he moved over to lay on top of me, and I went blind and numb with terror. His hard, muscled chest pressed down on me as his hands roamed under my shirt and over my breasts. A guy had never gone this far with me – not counting that time I hooked up briefly with Bex's cousin Rowan and did some heavy petting with him in a cabana. But that was the extent of it. Joe was going to forcefully go where no man had gone before, and I was powerless to stop him.

He pulled my shirt up and off and began working on my bra. *Please, Mary, Blessed Mother, whatever you call yourself, please help me. Please tell your son Jesus what this Protestant is going through. Please, and*

I promise to ask Lorraine to teach me to say a proper rosary in gratitude for your help. He succeeded in loosening my bra and began to pull it off as tears poured down my face.

At that moment, a bright light engulfed the interior of the car. Joe leaped up sharply from me, and I quickly arranged my clothing back to its original order. Sitting up, I saw a face peering into the driver's window. It was Bobby's, and he was livid.

V

"MOTHERFUCKER!" Bobby screamed as he flung the car door open, yanked Joe out, and threw him up against the car. "I'll kill you!" he screamed. I exited the car and saw that a considerable crowd had gathered. Danny, Nicky, Lynn, Carol, and some other kids from Titans were present and comprised our crew. Also present was the sinister office guy with his and Joe's crew, which consisted of a phalanx of other sinister guys in their early to mid-twenties. I didn't know how he had managed to marshal so many of his and Joe's henchmen on such short notice.

Joe pushed Bobby off him; he was surprisingly strong for such a wiry guy. "Yeah, punk? You know how I feel about Lorraine. I want her, and she's gonna be mine. You don't stand a chance against me." He snapped his fingers, and the sinister office guy appeared at his side. "Take her," he pointed at me, "and keep her with you." The sinister office guy walked around the car and quickly grabbed me; I was too petrified to run. He forcibly moved me over to where his crew was gathered and stood behind me holding both my arms in an iron grip. I attempted to squirm away from him, but he changed his tactics by wrapping his arms around me and holding me close. "Now try to get away," he growled in a heavy Southwest Philly accent. I stilled, for I was well and truly imprisoned.

"I'll fucking kill you! I swear to God I will!" Bobby cried.

Joe laughed. "There's no need for violence because here's how we're gonna settle it: we're gonna have a race. From here down to Bartram

Avenue and back. The first one to come back here wins. When I win, I get Lorraine."

"What makes you think she'll go with you?" Bobby asked.

"She'll have no choice. I'm taking her with me whether she wants to go or not. I plan on setting her up at my crib in Springfield and giving her the kind of life you'll never be able to. I've been planning this for a long time."

A murmur ran through Bobby's crew, and they looked at me, horrified. Lynn, Carol, and the other girls started crying. I sagged heavily against the sinister office guy, who chuckled into my ear and said, "Get ready for your new life, sweetheart."

"This is bullshit," Nicky said. "Let's just end this. Just give Lorraine back to us, and we'll go our merry way. We promise not to press charges or go to the police."

"Shut up, punk, this doesn't concern you," Joe snapped at him. "Me and your friend are gonna play this shit out." He turned to look at Bobby again. "Get in your car, loser," he commanded before turning to march to his car and climb inside it.

"Look, you can do this," Danny told Bobby encouragingly. "The Dart's got a powerful engine. It can blow that shitty Trans Am right out of the water." Joe revved his car's motor loudly, warning Bobby to get moving.

"Fuck," Bobby said, defeated. He climbed into the Dart, started the ignition, and glided to a stop across from Joe's car, which was poised at the starting line. Joe flashed the sinister office guy a look that galvanized him to action again. He hoisted me up and carried me as if I were a ragdoll. He walked with me in his arms toward the six-foot gap between the two cars and into it. The cars' engines reverberated in my head as he stood holding me. "Go!" he yelled, and the cars took off, enveloping the sinister office guy and me in a cloud of burnt rubber and car exhaust. The crowd screamed and cheered.

Back at the sidelines, the sinister office guy set me back on my feet and wrapped his arms around me again. I watched the cars until they became specks in the distance. When I could no longer see or hear them, I became nauseous with fear. It was ludicrous that my fate hinged on this car race, and I considered the possibility that Joe would win – or if he didn't, that he would refuse to concede defeat and carry me off regardless.

I ran through a worst-case scenario in my head: if Joe were to do that, I would have to contact Lorraine somehow and let her know where I was. I would also have the additional challenge of returning to Arnant once the identity switch was over; how would I manage that if I were incarcerated in Joe's home? Mrs. K. and Grandmom would certainly involve the police, and that was the last thing I wanted, considering I was an imposter and not the real Lorraine.

As I fretted over my dilemma, I saw the cars coming back; they had completed the turnaround at Bartram. Bobby was in the lead! I screamed and cheered, along with the rest of our crew, as the sinister office guy repeatedly told me to shut up. To my horror, Joe pulled ahead, and now they were neck-and-neck! Dear God, no! Please! So much depended on Bobby winning, more than anyone present realized!

Five feet before the finish line, Bobby pulled ahead and sailed over it. Our crew and I went wild! I was released from imprisonment and ran to the Dart. Bobby jumped out and ran to me, and we kissed as we had never kissed before. I cried and hugged him in relief, thanking God—and the Blessed Mother, too—that Bobby was okay and that I had escaped a harrowing fate.

Joe, however, was not going to give me up without a fight, just as I had suspected. He made a beeline for me but didn't get very far, for Bobby and our crew descended upon him and violently attacked him. Joe's crew, with the sinister office guy leading the charge, plunged into the battle. Lynn, Carol, the other girls, and I moved to the side to watch the roiling mass of flailing arms and legs. I couldn't see Bobby anywhere in the melee.

"C'mon, let's go before the cops get here," Lynn urged, and the gang of us migrated up Holstein towards 70th Street and back to Southwest Philly proper. It was a lengthy journey, but we had no choice but to take it, as sticking around at Holstein wasn't an option.

With the drama behind me, I processed everything that had happened, especially the terrifying incident in Joe's car. If I were Lorraine, I'd press kidnapping and sexual assault charges against him. But as I wasn't her, I couldn't take legal action against him. The most I could do was to steer clear of Titans in the future.

I also thought of Bobby, Danny, Nicky, and the rest of their crew and hoped they would be okay.

The girls kindly walked me to the front door of Lorraine's house. Nighttime had fully fallen by the time we arrived. They hugged me and told me to take care of myself. After they had departed, I proceeded to the payphone on The Avenue for my check-in with Lorraine. I wanted nothing more than to go into the house and stay there for the rest of the night, considering everything I had been through, but Lorraine was waiting for my call, and I had big news. Titans was dark and unoccupied when I got to The Avenue; the sinister office guy had followed instructions. Lorraine was going to be incredulous when I told her my story.

Indeed, she was. "Holy shit!" she said. "A drag race and a kidnapping and a rumble; I don't believe it!" I omitted the part about the sexual assault. There was no sense in alarming her.

"It was an event, all right," I said. "I'm tempted to write a book about it someday; it was unbelievable! I hope Bobby and the others are okay. The girls and I got out of there just as the gang fight started; I have no idea what happened after that. I'll call Bobby tomorrow and let you know the outcome."

"Okay, please do that. By the way, I don't think you should go back to Titans anymore."

"No, not anymore. I can't risk running into Joe again."

"Wish me luck. Stuart called me today and asked if I wanted to go to the Merion Cricket Club tomorrow and play mixed doubles with his sister Eunice and her husband, and I'm fucking nervous about it," she said.

I laughed. "You'll be fine, lovey. You learned a lot of tennis at boot camp, and with luck, you'll only have to play this one time. Gonna run now. It's been a real day. Love you lots!"

Chapter Sixteen

Lorraine

Stuart rolled up at ten the next morning, and I was waiting for him dressed all in white, just like Daven told me. I even had a white ribbon tied around my ponytail, and I held a tennis racket. We zoomed off to Merion with "Electric Avenue" by Eddy Grant playing on the radio. I spent hours the night before going over the notes I took on tennis during boot camp, and I was so anxious and nervous that I quietly prayed a Memorare so that the Blessed Mother could intercede for me and help me play a decent game.

I rarely prayed, but I prayed now because that's how scared I was of this match. It would have been even better if I had my rosary with me so I could keep it in my pocket for good luck. But my rosary was back at Bonnaffon Street, and even if I did have it at Arnant, I couldn't carry it if I was supposed to be Daven, who was a hardcore Protestant.

When we got to Merion, we parked, checked in at the clubhouse, and went over to the tennis courts. Eunice and her husband, Cullen Pentney, were already there. Eunice had dark hair just like Stuart's, and Cullen was tall and had blonde hair parted on the side and slicked down. He kind of looked like a department-store mannequin because he looked so stiff and formal.

After Stuart introduced me to them, he said, "We'll play just two games and not a full set. After all, this isn't Wimbledon!" We all laughed. Eunice, Cullen, and Stuart knew what Wimbledon was, obviously. I assumed it was some kind of tennis tournament, so I just went along with them and laughed, too.

The time had come, and my stomach twisted into a knot. Stuart stood at the baseline and told me to stand just in front of the service line. On the other side of the net, Cullen stood at the baseline, and Eunice at the service line. Stuart and Cullen were diagonal to each other, and so were me and Eunice. Stuart took a ball out of his pocket and served. It was on!

The ball flew past me and over to Cullen, who fired it back to Stuart. They volleyed for a little bit, then the ball flew over to Eunice, who fired it at me. Oh Jesus, I thought, please don't fail me now! I fired the ball back at Eunice, remembering everything Daven told me about forehand during tennis training at boot camp. I was relieved that the ball sailed over the net to her.

Then the ball came back to me, but I missed it. "Fifteen, love!" Cullen called out. I flashed a sad look to Stuart, but he seemed okay. He served the next ball. It flew over to Cullen, who swung and missed it. "Ace serve!" Stuart called out. "Fifteen-fifteen!"

The games lasted about an hour and a half. When they were all over, we tallied the scores. Eunice and Cullen won both of them, and I know the loss was my fault for being a sucky player. Maybe I shouldn't have been so hard on myself, because actually, I did great for someone who never played tennis before in their life.

"Sorry," I said to Stuart as we started packing up our rackets and other gear. "I haven't played in a while, and I'm rusty."

"Not to worry, darling. We'll simply have to play more games to get you back to your fighting weight."

"That's a wrap!" Eunice said as we began to walk off the court. "How about we do lunch at the café?" Everyone said yes to this idea, and I realized how hungry I was. We headed over to the cafe, which was packed with people, all of them dressed in solid white, and most of them having blond hair. They looked like angels who had floated down from heaven. I ordered a Cobb salad and a Coke.

As I ate, I noticed a girl staring right at me. She was blonde and had a very Main Line look. At first, I thought it was just a coincidence, that maybe she was staring at someone or something behind me. But then I saw her eyes dart to Stuart and then back to me, and her face grew red.

Eunice, who was sitting in pretty much the same direction I was, saw her, too.

She gave my hand a little tap under the table. "Would you gentlemen mind if we ladies took a quick trip to the bathroom to powder our noses?" she asked, and they said that was fine. We got up and made for the bathroom. It was one of those really fancy ones with a sitting room that had a little sofa, and she sat me down on it.

"I saw that blonde, too," she said. "It's not a coincidence that she's staring at you. Her name is Chandlee Singer, and she's from Wayne. She's Stuart's ex-girlfriend." I didn't know what to say; this was such a surprise. She went on. "He broke up with her during Memorial Day weekend, and she didn't take too well to it. He told me he couldn't stand her anymore, called her a shallow, self-centered blonde."

I was surprised by all this. It never occurred to me that Stuart had girlfriends in his past; it was something I just never thought about. But here was his ex, coughed up courtesy of the Merion Cricket Club.

"What should we do?" I asked. "Should we cut lunch short and leave?" Because honestly, if this Chandlee Singer was a spurned woman, I didn't want to be in the way of that!

"We'll finish quickly and gently push lunch along," she said. "I don't want to let Stuart know Chandlee's here. She'll put him in a bad mood very fast." I said okay, and we went back to the table. Stuart and Cullen were talking about something called Devon, and Cullen was saying that his sister competed in it this year in the Hunter category. I had no idea what they were talking about. Me and Eunice finished our food as fast as we could, and to make Stuart and Cullen hurry along, she said she really wanted to go shopping.

"I want to go to Suburban Square. I'd like to check out Strawbridge and Clothier. Daven wants to go, too."

"Ladies and their shopping!" Cullen laughed, and Stuart joined in. We called the waitress for the check, paid it, and left. We got in our cars; me and Stuart were going to follow Eunice and Cullen to

Suburban Square, which was an outdoor shopping mall just down the street. I had never been there and was excited to go, to be honest. But I couldn't act excited because Daven went there a lot, and it was nothing new to her.

As we pulled out of the parking lot, I just so happened to glance in the car's side mirror and saw the reflection of Chandlee Singer standing by her own car, throwing a look to us that could have killed.

Daven

The day after the "rumble," as Lorraine had called it during the previous night's conversation, Bobby showed up at the house with a black eye and a few cuts and bruises, but otherwise, he was okay. He was on foot, as the Dart had gotten a little banged up from the previous night's brouhaha and needed a few simple repairs. I had just returned from mass and was wearing the same blue dress I had worn the week before. I told Bobby to wait on the porch while I went inside to change into a T-shirt, shorts, and sneakers.

"I'd rather not talk here," he said when I rejoined him. "Let's go to the park." We proceeded to the park on Grays Avenue, the one we had visited a few weeks earlier on our first date. We sat on a bench and watched little kids on the swings.

"I beat the ever-living shit out of Joe," he said. "I fucked him up as hard as I could. And I'm glad you and the other girls got out of there when youse did. The fuzz showed up a few minutes after youse left; I dunno who called them. Me, Danny, Nicky, and the other guys got out of there fast. I don't know if Joe or any of his crew got away. I hope they all got busted."

"I'm staying out of Titans from now on," I said.

Bobby nodded his head. "That's the best thing to do. By the way, you should press charges against Joe for kidnapping."

I wanted to, but of course, I couldn't. "No, I'll let it go. It's not worth it, and I'm not barking up his tree."

"Did he hurt you?" he asked.

"No, all the damage was psychological. I'll be okay." I would keep the sexual assault to myself and never tell Bobby about it.

He wrapped his arm around me, held me close, and kissed me on the forehead. "I'd do anything to protect you, you know that."

"I know," I said. We cuddled briefly, and then he announced, "You want pizza? We can go to Pizza Villa if you want if you're okay with walking it." I said I was, and we made our way over.

Pizza Villa was about four blocks away at 67th and Dicks, a little corner joint with divine smells that hit us as soon as we entered. We ate delicious pizza, laughed, and had a great time. A pang went through me, knowing I would have to end it with Bobby when the identity switch was over. There was no guarantee that he and the real Lorraine would hit it off; breaking up would be the best course of action. I agonized over how to do that, but I pushed that thought aside. "Is There Something I Should Know?" by Duran Duran played on a boombox behind the store's counter, and I allowed Simon LeBon's voice to fill my head and displace thoughts of the heartbreaking reality that would hit in six weeks.

v

Before I went to bed that night, I extracted Lorraine's rosary from her nightstand drawer and prayed it the way she had taught me during our phone conversation. Even though praying a rosary violated my beliefs, I felt I should keep my promise to Jesus's mother for her help getting me out of a tough spot with Joe.

Chapter Seventeen

Lorraine

Me and Stuart saw our first movie together. It was *Staying Alive*, which was the sequel to *Saturday Night Fever*. We saw it at the Ardmore Theater in Ardmore, and it was its opening night, so the crowds were pretty big. It was okay. I wasn't big on dance movies, and it looked to me like it was trying to compete with *Flashdance*.

Stuart dropped me off at Arnant around ten that night. Consuelo was still awake; she was in the kitchen getting stuff ready for the next day's meals. I gave her an "*Hola*," but she just stared at me. I didn't know what was wrong, and I was picking up a funny vibe from her. But I didn't think too much about it. I prepared a bowl of cereal and carried it up to Daven's room, a little snack before I went to bed.

There was a message from Daven on her answering machine. I came home too late from the movie last night to talk to her, and we missed each other again tonight, too. I would have to catch her again tomorrow night.

As I ate my cereal and watched *Falcon Crest*, I thought back to the mixed doubles at the Merion Cricket Club and Chandlee Singer. It kind of creeped me out the way she stared at us as we were leaving. Eunice said Chandlee and Stuart's breakup wasn't a very smooth one, and I wondered if I would run into Chandlee again and what I would do if I did. I didn't say anything about her to Stuart.

I wondered about Stuart, too, and thought that I really liked him. What was I going to do when the identity switch ended? Could I just let the real Daven take over and hope she would hit it off with him? What would I tell him if I decided to break it off? I finished my cereal, brushed my teeth, and climbed into bed. I wouldn't let myself think of that now. As I fell asleep, I again saw the side mirror of Stuart's car with Chandlee in the reflection. It followed me into my dreams all night.

Daven

I took my first-ever trip to the MacDade Mall in Holmes, a little town in Delco, to see *Staying Alive* at the mall's cinema. This was the movie's opening night, and there were many people there, as it was the anticipated sequel to *Saturday Night Fever*. Before the movie started, we cruised the mall and checked out the stores. My favorite was an extremely trendy clothing store called Famous Maid. I bought a set of plastic bracelets that had a wavy shape; they were all the rage that summer.

After the movie was over, Bobby said, "Yo, let's stop in at the MacDade House; they're having a dance tonight." I agreed, and we drove down there; it was only a few blocks down the boulevard. We entered the building under a side entrance topped with a marquee. The scene was populated by a crowd of burnouts thrashing to "Lick It Up" by KISS.

A guy approached us and introduced himself to me as Mark. He was a friend of Bobby's from the neighborhood. "Lemme give you one of these," he said, handing Bobby a small square of white paper. It was a handbill announcing a battle of the bands due to perform in two weeks.

"Cool!" Bobby said. "We're definitely going to this. There's this one band called Deep Six that's going to be there. They'll probably win." He folded the handbill and slipped it into his back pocket. He asked if I wanted a soda, and we bought two Cokes and sipped them as we watched the kids dance up a storm to "Escalator of Life" by Robert Hazard, who, Bobby informed me, was a local guy who had grown up in Springfield. We couldn't resist the beat and began dancing to it, too.

v

"We're going out to dinner with Paulie and Deirdre next Saturday at Trieste," Mrs. K. announced one Saturday afternoon in the middle of July at Finnegan's pool. She, Grandmom, and I sat on beach chairs enjoying the sun and listening to "Wanna Be Startin' Somethin'" by Michael Jackson playing on the public address. I wanted to return to the pool but remained seated.

"That's great," I said, knowing a response was expected of me. Lorraine had told me so much about them, and I was interested in meeting them. I had never heard of the Trieste restaurant and was just as eager to visit it as I was to see Paulie and Deirdre.

They arrived at five on the designated day. Paulie was tall, about six feet, with brown hair that was a little long at the back and brushed his collar. He also had a thick mustache with a separation in the middle. He wore a blue dress shirt, gray pants, and black shoes. Dierdre was also tall and had a headful of fluffy, winged-back blonde hair. She wore a pink shirt dress with cap sleeves and a pair of Candies. The heels were so high that she teetered in them. They had a very typical Southwest Philly look. I could have trolled the neighborhood and found at least a dozen couples who looked just like them.

I smoothed down the white dress Lorraine had worn for her graduation. It had a ruffled bodice, leg-of-mutton sleeves, and a ruffled hem. Along with it, I wore the same white pumps she had worn to her graduation. It was the nicest dress she owned. I was taking a chance by wearing a white dress to an Italian restaurant because I knew the spaghetti sauce would fly everywhere, especially considering what a messy person I was! But it was the only dress Lorraine owned that was nice enough to wear to dinner. Mrs. K. and Grandmom were dressed in polyester blouses and slacks; both wore flat-heeled shoes.

We piled into Paulie's 1981 Camaro. It was black with a red stripe down its side, like a racing car, and I was sure it had seen its share of action in many races. Paulie and Deirdre sat up front; I sat in the back, sandwiched between Mrs. K. and Grandmom. Paulie revved the motor, and off we sped up the street, onto The Avenue, and into Delco. "Let's Dance" by David Bowie blasted from the car's stereo as we drove.

Trieste was located on Chester Pike in a town in Delco called Prospect Park. It wasn't a long drive; we were there in less than twenty minutes. We parked at the lot across the street and crossed over to the restaurant, Paulie with his hand under Dierdre's elbow to keep her steady. We walked into a rustic-looking dining room with a Frank Sinatra song playing somewhere in the background. The intermingling aromas of spaghetti sauce and Italian food crossed my nose, and they were tantalizing! Paulie gave our reservation name to the hostess, and we were seated in the back of the restaurant in a large booth adjacent to the bar. Paulie and Dierdre sat together on one side, and just like the car ride, I was sandwiched between Mrs. K. and Grandmom on the other.

After the waitress had taken our drink order, Grandmom started the conversation. "Paulie and Deirdre, it's good to see youse. How's the auto-parts store? How's hairdressing school?"

Paulie's face split into a broad grin. "Things are all right at my job. I might get a promotion. Assistant manager!" Mrs. K. and Grandmom gasped simultaneously, and Deirdre gave a big grin that said she was proud of her man and knew he would pull off such a feat. I smiled, proud of him, too, even though I knew very little about him.

"Well, that's great!" Mrs. K. beamed. "Deirdre, hon, how's it going with you?"

"One more year, and I'll be finished with hairdressing school. I'm already looking at which salons I'd like to work."

"Ah, I'm so proud of youse. And there are lots of hair salons in Southwest that you can work at," Grandmom said as she lit a cigarette. I turned away from it to keep the smoke out of my face as much as I could. The waitress arrived with our drinks, and I immediately sipped my Diet Coke. She took our order and disappeared again.

"Lorraine," Deirdre said, "your mom tells me you're looking into going to Katharine Gibbs." I pretended to look indignant as I glared at Mrs. K., remembering Lorraine's complaints against being coerced to go there. Mrs. K. gave me a blank stare and took another sip of her vodka and tonic.

"Yeah, maybe," I replied sulkily. "I'm not sure what I'm doing yet."

"Indecisive and with no drive, just like your goddamn father," Mrs. K. retorted. "At least you're not like him, Paulie. You're going places."

"Yeah, I'd like to make store manager someday, but I need my high-school diploma for that."

"I keep telling him to get his GED," Deirdre chimed in, and Paulie's exasperated look told me they had argued about this topic many times.

I was emboldened to respond. "Tell you what, Mom," I told Mrs. K. "I'll go to Katharine Gibbs if Paulie gets his GED. How does that sound?" I think this was precisely what Lorraine would have said in this situation, so I went with it.

She cackled. "Sure, that works for me, although I don't think you'll do it even then."

Our appetizer arrived: an order of fried apples. I had never eaten them before, and I liked them. As I ate, the others continued the conversation. The waitress cleared our appetizer course, and shortly afterward, our entrees arrived. I had ordered eggplant parmigiana, something else I had never eaten before. I had never eaten much Italian food save for pizza and spaghetti. When my family ate out, the Italian food we ate was very elegant and authentic, food that looked as if it could have come straight from Italy. Working-class Italian cuisine was uncharted territory, as was everything else in Lorraine's world.

I took a bite of eggplant parmigiana, and it was delicious! It melted in my mouth! It was served on a bed of spaghetti covered in the best spaghetti sauce I had ever tasted! It was a shame that my parents would never dare set foot in this restaurant because it was not only working-class Italian cuisine but also located on the "poor" side of town, meaning south of Route One. I resolved to return here someday, after the summer and the identity switch were over.

The conversation revolved around trivial matters that I can't recall. But I do recall them talking about the Phillies' promising season and their potential to go to the World Series. They also talked about the upcoming mayoral election in Philadelphia.

"I can't believe Frank Rizzo was defeated in the primary," Grandmom said. "That guy Wilson Goode is going to run on the Democratic ticket."

"We might have a black mayor," Mrs. K. said. "Who'da thought? It feels like Rizzo's been mayor forever."

"Maybe he'll make things better," Deirdre added hopefully. "There are so many problems in the city."

Paulie laughed. "I think he's gonna set things on fire!"

Dessert came, and I ordered rice pudding and hot tea. They were delicious, just as the other courses had been. The check came. Paulie paid it, and we trooped out of the restaurant, back to his car, and back to Southwest Philly. When we arrived, Deirdre pulled off her Candies and changed into a pair of flats before leaving the car. I followed Paulie, Mrs. K., and Grandmom into the house, but Deirdre tugged at my arm.

"Come for a walk with me," she said, almost imploringly, it seemed to me. I told her I would as soon as I changed into more comfortable shoes, as the white pumps weren't suitable for long walks. I ran into the house and changed into a pair of white moccasins I found in Lorraine's closet; they were the only shoes she owned that I could get away with wearing with this dress. I returned to the sidewalk, where Deirdre was waiting. We walked down the street towards Paschall Avenue.

"We haven't talked in a while," Deirdre said.

"No," I agreed, "we haven't." At least, I assumed Lorraine and Deirdre hadn't talked in a while. All I could do was play along.

"I wanted to talk to you after your graduation dinner. But a lot was going on, and your mom and grandmom were so excited and making such a big fuss over you that I couldn't find an opportunity to pull you away. And I can see why: you're the first one in your family to graduate from high school. You've made a big splash! I wish Paulie would get a move on with finishing his education. I keep bugging him about it because, like he said back there, getting his GED could mean a bigger promotion and more money for us."

"I could talk to him if you want me to," I said. But I didn't want to have to do that. Being in the role I was, that of an imposter, I didn't want to put fingers in any more pies than I had to.

She sighed. "No, don't worry about it. I'll try to make him come around. It's just frustrating." We rounded the corner onto Paschall Avenue, and I felt she wanted to discuss more than Paulie and his procrastinating ways. We walked down to the Paschall Variety, the same store at which Bobby, the others, and I had bought lighters for the Stevie Nicks concert. The same dark-haired teenage boy in the West Catholic T-shirt stood behind the counter. "She Works Hard for the Money" by Donna Summer played from the boombox this time. Remembering the neighborhood etiquette Lorraine had taught me, I took a dollar out of my little handbag and asked him for quarters, which he promptly slid across the counter.

I scooped them up and walked to the Centipede machine on the opposite wall. I dropped a quarter in and challenged Deirdre to a game. We laughed and cheered each other on during the competition. She was a better player than I was and achieved a higher score. I suspected she had honed her video-game skills by spending considerable time playing them.

After the game, she treated me to Frank's black-cherry Wishniak soda and bought one for herself. We walked out of the corner store, but instead of continuing down the street, she cut a sharp right turn around the corner and leaned up against the side of the building. I would have directed us to sit on the curb, just as I had seen so many Southwest Philly kids do, but we were in our dress clothes and couldn't.

"Lorraine, thanks for being a good friend to me. You're more of a sister to me than my own sister is," she said, after a long drag on her soda can.

"You're welcome," was all I could say. Lorraine had told me that Deirdre was a sweet girl who had always been kind to her, and I could tell that this was true.

"I'm sorry for ragging about Paulie. But it would really help us if he could someday be promoted to store manager, and not having his GED is really holding him back." I had the feeling this was a secondary issue that was underpinning a larger one. I waited for her to go on as I sipped my soda. Two boys in our age group sauntered by. They were clad in the typical burnout fashion of concert shirts, jeans, and high-topped Nikes. They looked bemused to see two girls in their finery leaning up against a wall. They made no remarks and kept walking.

"Keep this to yourself, but me and Paulie visited your dad last week," she said. "Paulie's been giving him money. He and his girlfriend are both on disability, and it's hard for them."

"Are they okay?"

"Yeah, aside from their struggles. They're still living in that camper in the Pine Barrens." She took another sip of soda. "That's one reason I want to keep bringing more money into the house. I think we'll have to keep helping them as time goes by. I don't see an end to their struggle."

As we sipped our sodas, I knew there was more Deirdre wanted to tell me. After a few minutes of silence, she opened her mouth to speak, then quickly slapped her hand across it. Shoving her can of soda at me, she bolted to a trash can that stood several feet away from us and vomited into it. I stood in alarm, wishing there was something I could do.

When she finished heaving, she staggered back over to me. "And there's one more thing I want to tell you," she panted. "I'm pregnant. Paulie doesn't know it yet."

Chapter Eighteen

Daven

I was struck dumb by Deirdre's revelation. Given the subtle urgency she had displayed since we had returned from Trieste, I should have seen this coming.

"That's another reason why I want Paulie to advance to store manager and bring in more money," she explained. "We're going to need it for the baby."

"How far along are you?" I asked.

"Maybe about six weeks. When I saw you at your graduation, I wanted to tell you that I thought I was pregnant. Now I know it for sure."

"You need to get to a doctor soon," I said.

"Yeah, I know. But I have to tell Paulie first, and then I have to wait for his benefits to kick in once he's promoted to assistant manager."

She was in a real pickle, and I felt sorry for her. Her eyes glistened with unshed tears. I fished in my handbag, found a tissue, and handed it to her.

"Thank you," she sobbed as she dabbed her eyes with it, blue mascara running down her face. "I'm really scared, Lorraine. This is too much for me. I don't know how to break it to Paulie, and with him giving money to your dad and his girlfriend, this is going to hit us so hard."

I put my arm around her. "It'll be all right. Just talk to him. Do it tonight! The sooner you do it, the sooner you can devise a plan to make it all work."

"Yeah, I know, I have to do that. All right, I'll do it tonight as soon as we get home. I don't know what I'd do without you. I'm lucky to have you as my almost-sister; I really am. I wanna marry Paulie someday, especially with the baby coming. And I want you to be my maid of honor."

I almost started crying, too. "Thank you," I whispered.

I finished my soda as she finished hers. I collected the empty cans and threw them in the trash can. "Come on, let's get back to the house. They'll wonder where we've been," I said. We turned and walked back to Bonnaffon Street. A car drove by playing "Sweet Dreams" by The Eurythmics. I sang it softly as she and I returned to Lorraine's home.

v

During my check-in call to Lorraine that night, I blurted the news. "You're going to be an aunt!" I cried. I talked to her on another payphone on The Avenue, across the street from the Paschalville Library. I no longer felt safe using the payphone near Titans.

"Are you serious?" she screeched.

"Yes! According to Deirdre, she's due at the end of February. How exciting for you! But she hasn't told Paulie yet," I added.

"Oh, my God, this is awesome! I'm going to be an aunt!" she cried.

"There's more. Paulie and Deirdre recently visited your dad and his girlfriend. Deirdre said they're both on disability and not doing well financially, so Paulie's been giving them money. She's concerned about the expenditures, especially with the baby on the way."

"Is my dad okay?" she asked anxiously.

"Basically, yes. He seems more indigent than anything else. That means poor," I added with a chuckle.

"That's good to know. Thanks for the updates. I'm gonna let you go now. Talk to you tomorrow."

"Same here. Have a good sleep!"

Lorraine

I was swimming in Arnant's pool one hot, sunny afternoon when Consuelo called out to me, "*Señorita* Daven, is for you!" I thanked her as she gave me another one of her funny looks. She handed me the phone, and it was Stuart.

"Hello, darling," he said in that sexy Main Line accent of his. "Just thought I'd let you know that I made a reservation for us for next Friday night at Le Bec-Fin for seven. I'll come in a limo for you at six. I know we'll have a smashing time!" This was that fancy-schmancy restaurant he told me about a few weeks back. I was excited but nervous at the same time. I would have to remember all the table manners that Daven taught me. Not only that, but I didn't know what I'd wear. Me and Stuart talked for a few more minutes before we hung up. I went back to the pool and spread out on the floating chaise lounge. I would make sure I told Daven about Le Bec-Fin during that night's call.

v

"We're going to Le-Bec Fin next Friday night!" I told Daven as soon as she called.

"That's fabulous! Do you remember your table manners?"

"Yeah, I wrote them in my notebook. But what should I wear? I've never been to a place this nice in my life!"

"You'll find a black dress and a sequined black shawl in my closet. Wear them along with a pair of black heels. I have a small black dress purse you can carry, too. You're going to have a great time!"

"Do you and Bobby have anything planned anytime soon?" I asked.

"We're going to a Battle of the Bands show at the MacDade House next Sunday."

"You'll love it! The MacDade has the best cover bands! Well, I'm going to end it here. You have a good night."

v

The limo pulled up to Arnant at six. Stuart hopped out to help me inside as I awkwardly navigated myself in Daven's tight black dress and heels, all the while keeping the shawl level so it wouldn't trip me. He was smartly dressed in a suit and tie, and of course, he looked foxy, as always. The guy was a total dreamboat. Once we were settled, the driver whisked us along Lancaster Avenue and the Schuylkill Expressway to 15th and Walnut Streets in Center City.

It was my first time in a limo, and I was so excited! It was so big and roomy, with space for at least six people. Stuart told me to put a song on the stereo. Of course, I wanted to tune into 94 WYSP but I knew it would be out of character for Daven to do that, so I put on 98 WCAU instead, which is what she'd probably listen to. "Human Touch" by Rick Springfield began to play. The song filled the whole limo. I couldn't believe how awesome that stereo was.

Stuart helped me out of the limo when it pulled up to the restaurant. It was the fanciest place I'd ever seen. Over the door was a curved metal canopy with LE-BEC FIN written on it in fancy writing. Underneath it was a glass door framed in gold. But the crazy thing was that there was a sign requesting that you ring the doorbell to be admitted, with the word *Merci* at the bottom. I assumed that word was French. God, I hoped I wouldn't have to speak French there! Stuart rang the bell, the door buzzed, and we walked in.

A maître d' stood in a tuxedo at the podium right in front of us. He said, *"Bon soir,"* which I assumed meant "Good evening." Stuart gave his name and reservation info, and the maître d' escorted us into the dining room. It looked like a palace! The walls were painted gold and decorated with long mirrors, and the chairs were gold, too. The tables had white linen tablecloths – I never ate in a place that had tablecloths – and on top of them were fine silverware, dishes, and glasses. Beautiful glass chandeliers hung from the ceilings, but what grabbed my attention the most was the gold fireplace, which was topped by another mirror, this one fancier than the others. A floral arrangement sat on the fireplace's mantle. And believe it or not, we were going to sit at the table right in front of it!

Everything Daven taught me about eating in a fancy restaurant came rushing through my head. Sure enough, Stuart pulled my chair out and helped me slide in. I put my napkin in my lap right away. Then Stuart sat in his chair, and the maître d' handed us menus and walked away.

Another guy, also in a tuxedo, walked up to us and asked if we wanted wine. Because I was too young to drink, Stuart declined. And it was a good thing, because I would have been very tempted!

Next came our waiter. Stuart ordered a big bottle of Perrier water for us to drink. I never had Perrier and was eager to try it. The waiter came back with a big green bottle, and he poured it for us. Perrier tasted just like seltzer water to me.

Some of the words on the menu were written in French. I was afraid to ask Stuart for a translation because Daven probably already knew French, so I went with it. He asked what I wanted for the first course, which was under the category called *Les Entrées*. Something called *Galette de Crabe* caught my eye; I figured anything with crab had to be good. So that's what we ordered. A few minutes later, it came: they were crab cakes, but fancier. They were in a cream sauce and served with a side of green beans. They were delicious!

The waiter cleared the plates and utensils for that course and asked what our next course would be. It was *poissons*, which was seafood. We ordered scallops in a grape-flavored syrup topped with pumpkin seeds.

Next came the *intermezzo*, which was a dollop of lemon sorbet that Stuart told me cleansed your palate for the next course, which was *viandes*, or meat. He ordered the lamb, and I got the chicken, which came with these greens called Swiss chard and these funny-looking mushrooms called chanterelles. But it was delicious!

The cheese course was next, followed by more sorbet. The very last course was a thing of glory: a dessert cart! It was two levels of pure sin! My head spun as the waiter explained all the desserts to us. Stuart got the apple tart, and I got a rich chocolate cake called *gateau*. We both ordered coffee. It was so good, and it was the brewed kind, not the crappy instant kind my mother always bought.

I was sad when that dinner was over because it was the best of my life! The waiter presented the check. Stuart put his American Express card in the little book that the check came in, and the waiter processed it. He signed the slip and put the book on the table. He held my chair out for me as I got up, and we left the restaurant to wait at the curb for our limo, which was going to pull up in a few minutes.

As it glided up to us, a lady, who had just come out of Le Bec-Fin, rushed up to us as we were about to get inside. "Daven Barrett!" she said. She was dressed as fancy as I was and wore a lot of expensive jewelry. This was obviously someone Daven knew, so I played it off like I knew exactly who she was.

"Hi!" I said. "Good to see you!"

"It's me, Bootsie, your mother's canasta partner. You probably don't recognize me all decked out like this!" Thank God, she gave me a clue! "It's wonderful to see you here! Why aren't you in Longport with your parents?"

"Truthfully, Bootsie, I've had a long and busy year and needed time to rest. Finishing school in Switzerland, the deb ball, the charity ball, endless college interviews..."

"You poor thing! Your mother said you were having a busy year. What college did you decide on?"

"Vassar."

"Wonderful! My sister went there! Good heavens, where are my manners?" She turned to the man at her side and introduced him to Stuart as her husband Aldan, who insisted we call him Trip. I then introduced Stuart to them.

"Well, we'd best be going," Trip said as their limo pulled up behind ours. "It was nice to bump into you, Daven, and nice to meet you, Stuart." We waved goodbye as they climbed in and glided off. Then we climbed into our limo and glided off, too. It was a wonderful night.

Chapter Nineteen

Daven

At the end of July, we set off to see The Battle of the Bands at the MacDade House. We piled into the Dart, and I rode shotgun with Bobby as Danny, Nicky, Lynn, and Carol sat in the back seat packed together in a tight bunch. We arrived and walked into a dimly-lit interior with red, diamond-shaped fixtures glowing on the wall. Beneath them on the stage a band was setting up their equipment, the name Deep Six splashed across the bass drum.

The patrons were filing in, all of them dressed in an array of concert shirts, sleeveless shirts, jeans, high-topped sneakers, Spandex, bandanas, and lots and lots of feathered hair. I didn't look out of place at all in Lorraine's shiny lavender polyester shirt, designer jeans, and high-topped sneakers, nor did Bobby in his dark-orange Philadelphia Stars T-shirt, jeans, and high-topped Nikes. Our friends, like us, were attired similarly to the patrons.

After about half an hour, the band had finished their set-up, and more patrons arrived. The loud buzz of feedback filled the big room as the guitarist plucked a few notes on his instrument. The crowd began to cheer, yell, and whistle as the lead singer, a guy dressed in a green-and-black tiger-striped shirt and green spandex pants, approached the microphone and greeted the crowd, which shouted back a greeting to him.

The notes thundered out of the amps, and as the tune picked up momentum, I recognized it right away. It was one of the metal songs Lorraine insisted I know, but its name wouldn't come to me. As the lead singer yelled the lyrics into the microphone, recognition dawned. It was a cover of Judas Priest's "You've Got Another Thing Coming." The crowd screamed its delight and began to thrash wildly to the music. Bobby and our friends whooped their approval as he grabbed my hand and encouraged me to dance along with him.

The band performed several more metal covers. Some of the songs I knew, some I didn't. And although this music wasn't to my taste, I had a lot of fun anyway dancing with Bobby. At the end of one of the covers, a guy in a concert shirt and jeans who was standing in the front row looked at me and waved. I had no clue who he was, but I knew better than to give him a blank stare. He was probably someone Lorraine knew, meaning I should know him. I smiled and waved back. In a few seconds, much to my dread, he bounded over to me.

"Yo, Lor!" he said. "Don't tell me you don't remember me."

No, I don't, I wanted to say. But instead, I put on a big smile and said, "Yeah, but I can't remember your name."

"Mike Miller from 67th and Linmore. We worked at the McDonald's on The Avenue together last year. Remember that night when we closed together, and we got drunk off a bottle of vodka that we hid in the ice machine?"

"Oh yeah! How are you? It's good to see you." I introduced him, Bobby, and the others but dared not say anything else out of fear of revealing my cluelessness.

"Man, I got so hammered on that shit. I puked my guts up right outside my front door when I got home."

"Sorry to hear that. How've you been?"

"Yeah, after I quit, I took a job in Delco, driving a truck for a contractor."

"Oh, that's good that you found something," I said. I wanted him to end the conversation and go away, but he looked at me expectantly, and I realized he wouldn't do that until I gave him a rundown of my life.

"Yeah, well, I quit there a few months ago when that dickhead manager grabbed my ass. I walked right out. I'm not doing nothin' now, just killin' time. My mom wants me to go to secretary school now that high school's done, but I dunno."

"Okay, well, best of luck, and great seeing you again, Lor!" To Bobby and the others, he added, "Nice meeting you!" He sauntered away and resumed his spot in the first row, and I heaved a sigh of relief.

"I hope he didn't know that I didn't remember him. He didn't leave much of an impression," I said to Bobby, laughing nervously.

Deep Six finished their set, and the audience applauded them wildly. They departed the stage, and the next contestant appeared, a band called Holy Angel. They, too, were donned in the requisite Spandex and sported the requisite hair. The audience applauded again, and the lead singer shouted hello and launched into their song. It was a cover of Sammy Hagar's "Your Love is Driving Me Crazy," and everyone went wild! Even though metal wasn't to my taste, this song was a terrific, high-energy ballad!

The event wrapped up around midnight, with Deep Six declared the winner. We piled back into the Dart and returned to Southwest Philly. Bobby dropped off the others at their homes, and then he and I drove to the athletic field at the end of Elmwood Avenue. We parked alongside it in the darkness. He put on the radio but didn't have to flip around to find an appropriate song, for "Making Love Out of Nothing at All" by Air Supply played as soon as he turned it on.

"God, Lorraine, I love you so much," he said as his mouth came down on mine. I held back my tears, knowing that a heartbreaking end would be inevitable.

PART THREE

August 1983

Chapter Twenty

Daven

"Guess what?" Mrs. K said the next night, after a phone call from Paulie. "Paulie and Deirdre are expecting at the end of February! I'm gonna be a grandmom!" Grandmom and I cried out, too. Of course, it was all an act on my part, as I already knew this.

"We have to plan a baby shower for Deirdre in a few months," Grandmom pointed out. "Lorraine, you'll have to help with it, too."

"Yeah, sure," I said. "I'd be glad to." I was saddened that I would be long out of the picture by the time the shower rolled around and wouldn't see Deirdre again. I had grown fond of her in the brief time I spent with her after the Trieste dinner.

I was fond of all Lorraine's family and friends, including Mrs. K. and Grandmom, as crude and dysfunctional as they were. I was going to miss them when the identity switch ended. My fondness for these Southwest Philadelphians and my dismay over my inevitable departure were things I hadn't anticipated when I proposed the identity switch.

Since Bobby was working, and Titans was forever off-limits, there was nothing for me to do. To fill my time, I grabbed Lorraine's Walkman and sat on the front porch listening to it. "Maniac" by Michael Sembello pumped into my ears. I focused on the light at the end of the tunnel, and what it would mean for me when everything ended in three weeks.

"Jersey tomatoes!" barked a voice over a loudspeaker, which I could hear even through my headphones. I had no idea what it was until I saw an old station wagon rolling down the street with a speaker mounted on its roof. "Watermelon! Corn! Peaches!" the voice barked again. Grandmom and Mrs. K. came out of the house with money in their hands, and I turned off the Walkman, took it off, and set it down.

"The huckster's here!" Grandmom said as she dragged her oxygen tank down the steps and out to the street with Mrs. K. behind her. Curious, I followed them as they walked to the back of the station wagon. The tailgate was open to reveal a bountiful display of fruits and vegetables. Above them dangled a scale mounted to the station wagon's ceiling. Mrs. K. piled peaches into it, and the huckster observed the weight and charged her accordingly. They also weighed and paid for corn and tomatoes. Other neighbors came to buy the produce, and soon, a sea of Southwest Philadelphians surrounded me, all chattering away in their distinct accents. I was never going to forget this world.

Lorraine

Me and Stuart drove for what seemed like forever to the Brandywine Polo Club, which was off Route One in Toughkenamon, a town in Chester County not too far from the Maryland state line. I'd never been out that way in my life; I thought I was traveling to the end of the earth. It was a hot and sunny day, perfect for an outdoor sport like polo. When I told Daven the night before that I was going to a polo match, she told me to wear her floppy white hat with a Lilly Pulitzer sundress and a pair of sandals. She told me not to wear heels because they would sink into the dirt and that flats were better for divot-stomping, whatever that was. Stuart wore a white sports jacket, light-blue button-down shirt, white pants, white loafers, and a straw boater hat. He looked like he should be selling ice cream.

When we got there, the parking lot was almost full. Stuart parked the Jaguar, and then we walked over to the ticket booth, where he handed in our tickets. "We're going to meet up with a few friends of mine," he said as he looked around. "They should be here any minute." A few minutes later, a guy and a girl showed up. He introduced them to me as Chaz Kenworth and Keating Masterson. All four of us then walked to the grandstand and sat near the top.

The crowd quieted down when the players rode up to the field on their horses. There were four of them on each team. They were numbered one through four, and they lined up in numerical order, each team facing the other. An umpire came out and rolled a white ball between them, and the game got started.

Polo was almost as confusing as cricket. To me, it looked like ice hockey played on horses. Stuart and his friends were really into it.

"Oh, too bad, Number Four, you were hooked!" Stuart yelled out when player Number Four tried to score a goal but his mallet – that's what Stuart called that hammer thing the players used to whack the ball – was blocked by a player on the other team.

Halftime came, and everybody got up. "Time to stomp the divots!" Chaz said, and we all moved toward the field and used our feet to push down the small mounds of dirt that the horses' hooves kicked up during the game. I told Stuart I was thirsty, and he said he would buy us some sodas. But I offered to go, so he gave me money, and off I headed to the concession stand.

As I was coming back, I saw her: Chandlee Singer, Stuart's ex-girlfriend that I saw at the restaurant at the Merion Cricket Club. I froze, the sodas dripping in my hands. She was dressed a lot like I was, in a floppy hat and a flowered sundress. She moved closer to me, and I saw that she had cold, light-blue eyes, which narrowed as she took me in.

"You know who I am, don't you?" she snapped.

"Yes, I know your name's Chandlee Singer. You're Stuart's ex-girlfriend."

She snorted. "That nosey fucking Eunice must have clued you in." Then she barked out a nasty laugh. "And you're his perfect little Daven. I've heard a lot about you. You're a dull little thing, aren't you?"

I didn't know what to say to this. The sodas kept dripping, and they were making my dress wet. But I was too afraid to move.

"Don't get too comfortable with him, darling. I'm winning him back any way I have to. You're not going to stand in my way, and neither is your pissant family. I'm sure we'll meet again." She marched past me, shoving me out of the way with her shoulder.

Stuart came rushing up to me, his face red, as Chandlee moved away from me. "Damn! I should have known she'd be here! Darling, I must be honest with you and tell

you – "

"I know who she is. I didn't want to tell you this, but Chandlee was at the Merion Cricket Club the same day we were. I noticed her during lunch. You didn't see her because your back was to her. Eunice told me about her when we went to the bathroom."

"Damn! That incorrigible harpy – Chandlee, that is! Has she said anything to upset you?"

I had to hold back my laughing when he said, "Incorrigible harpy." I would have used stronger words to describe Chandlee. "No, I'm fine. I won't let anything rain on today's parade." He smiled as he took one of the Cokes from me and chugged it as we walked back to the grandstand to rejoin Chaz and Keating. We got back to our seats for the next chukka, or period. It was a pretty exciting one. A member of the opposing team crossed the line of the ball. A foul was declared, which meant our team got a goal. Stuart and his friends went crazy!

The game was over in a few hours, and the four of us went back to Llanwyn to chill out and drink Lowenbrau. Me and Keating talked for a little bit. She mostly asked me about stuff pertaining to Daven's family, and I answered her questions the way Daven would have. I think Daven would have been proud of me, actually. I think I was getting this Main Line thing down pretty good.

Chapter Twenty-One

Lorraine

Bex called me the day after the polo match, all giggly. She wanted to know if I wanted to go shopping with her and Jensen at Suburban Square. I said yes, and an hour later, they pulled up to Arnant, and off we went.

I saw what Daven meant when she said that even though Bex and Jensen were her best friends, they sometimes excluded her from things. I didn't like how the two of them walked ahead of me and chitchatted, completely acting as if I wasn't there. I felt like a third wheel. As dishonest as this identity switch was, maybe it was a good thing because it was giving me and Daven a true best friend for each of us. I could plainly see that Bex and Jensen weren't real good friends for Daven.

We went to Strawbridge and Clothier and looked at most of their departments. When we got bored there, we left and walked out to the plaza and went to a boutique called Asta De Blue. They bought dresses, but I didn't buy anything because I wouldn't be able to keep it. When we finished there, we walked over to the Benetton store, where they bought matching shirts and pants. They didn't ask if I wanted to buy a matching outfit.

Finally, we were done shopping, and we had lunch at a deli called the Deli Garden. They didn't include me in their conversation all that much, and I wondered why they even bothered to include me in this shopping trip at all. I was so happy when they said they would take me home. Frankly, they were annoying, and I hoped it would be the last time I would see them.

Back at Arnant, I had dinner and watched TV afterward. Daven's call came while I was watching *Joanie Loves Chachi*. She gushed about all the fun she was having hanging out with Bobby and his friends on the corner and drinking Bud as they listened to 94 WYSP on the boombox. I was happy that she was experiencing a good life in Southwest Philly and happy also to have her as a best friend. Because, to be honest, I think she needed me way more than I needed her – and I needed her a lot.

Daven

I awoke one morning to realize I hadn't seen much of Southwest Philly, only Lorraine's neighborhood, a portion of The Avenue, Finnegan's pool, and Holstein Avenue. I wanted to see more of its attractions before the identity switch ended. I found her bicycle in the basement and used it for a tour. It was a fascinating area, with pizza shops, steak shops, hair salons, corner stores, churches, and block after block of rowhomes.

The churches were my favorite. In addition to St. Clement's, I visited three others, and they were all very lovely to look at: St. Barnabas, Our Lady of Loreto, and St. Mary of Czestochowa. I think there were a few more churches than these in Southwest Philly, but these were the closest and, therefore, the easiest to visit.

On the same block as Our Lady of Loreto was a bakery, Mattera's, baking the most heavenly rolls I had ever smelled! I can't even describe the smell, for it was so divine! A few blocks up from Mattera's, on Elmwood Avenue, was another bakery called Durso's that sold pastries. Their offerings were also divine! I could get fat living in that neighborhood because of all the excellent food surrounding me.

I pedaled down Elmwood Avenue and saw what Lorraine had told me was the General Electric factory. This imposing brick building towered seven stories above Southwest Philly like a castle. Next, I came to Island Avenue and a network of trolley tracks, and it was here that I turned around and returned to Bonnaffon.

Later, after dinner, Mrs. K. told me, "Lorraine, go down the cellar and get the baby stroller." I didn't ask why. I rose, walked to the cellar door, and flipped on the light, the rickety steps groaning under my weight as I descended. There was junk everywhere, and the cellar reeked of mothballs. I pushed aside cardboard boxes, tools, piles of clothes, and old furniture as I searched in vain for the stroller. I must have been taking too long because, after a few minutes, Mrs. K. called down to me, "Lorraine, what are you doing, building it?"

"I can't find the stroller," I called up.

"It's in the back of the cellar, next to the hot-water heater." I walked to the back of the cellar and found the stroller where she had said it was. It was so dim back there that I wasn't surprised I hadn't seen it at first. It was an ancient thing, probably left over from when Lorraine was a baby. I pulled it out and wheeled it backward up the stairs and into the kitchen. What in the world did Mrs. K. want with a stroller?

"Time to go trash-picking. Tomorrow's trash day, so everyone's trash is out tonight," Mrs. K. announced. Trash-picking? What did that mean? I followed her to the front door, still wheeling the stroller, with Grandmom in tow, wheeling her oxygen tank. After Mrs. K. locked the door behind us, we proceeded down the street as she took charge of the stroller. As we strolled along, I noticed neighbors peering at the piles of trash and refuse lined up along the sidewalk. Some were picking through them and producing items they carried off, and more than one neighbor pushed a baby stroller, like we did.

"Lorraine, look at that pile," she indicated, pointing to a pile right next to us. "Tell me if you see anything good." This was the most abominable thing I had ever done, as the last thing I wanted to do was touch someone else's trash, but touch it, I did. I opened a few trash cans and peered and poked inside, but I saw nothing except bags of trash. We moved on, and she directed me to examine more trash. I found nothing worth taking until we got to the end of the block, where we hit the jackpot: we found an old lamp, a colander, and a small nightstand all in the same pile. Mrs. K. and Grandmom loaded the lamp and the colander into the baby stroller. The nightstand wouldn't fit, so I had to carry it.

Grandmom chuckled as we crossed the street to examine the trash on that side, "This is great! That nightstand will look good in the living room!" As we sifted through a pile of trash, I saw a blur in the corner of my eye. Suddenly, hands were tugging at the nightstand. The hands belonged to an overweight, middle-aged woman with messy hair, bad skin, and bad teeth. She tugged on the nightstand with all her might as I tugged back, playing a tug-of-war with me in the middle of the neighborhood!

"Gimme that!" she screeched. "Youse already got enough! Save some for the rest of us!" I didn't know for how long I could fend her off when Mrs. K. jumped into the fray and gave the nightstand a good, hard yank away from her. "Piss off, Dottie, we found it first!" Grandmom barked obscenities at Dottie, as did Mrs. K., and soon all the neighbors were watching us. Some were too horrified to speak; others were rooting for Dottie or Mrs. K.

"Shut the fuck up, all of youse!" Mrs. K. screamed at them as she raced back to the house. She hugged the nightstand tightly to her body as Grandmom and I trailed behind her; she wheeled her oxygen tank, and I the stroller. We were soon back inside with our spoils, and Mrs. K. locked the door. I wouldn't have put it past that mob to rush into the house, with Dottie leading the charge!

Mrs. K. directed me to set up the nightstand in a corner of the living room. She fetched furniture polish and a cloth and cleaned the nightstand well. "There, it looks good as new!" she declared. It did look very nice. It was a little table about two feet tall in wood that looked like oak, but I'm sure it wasn't real. It had a small drawer at the top and a shelf at the bottom.

"What will we keep in it?" Grandmom asked.

"I dunno, extra cigarettes, maybe," Mrs. K. said. "Lorraine, open that drawer. Let's take a look at how much space it has." I complied, slowly sliding the drawer open, and a swarm of cockroaches poured out! There must have been at least a hundred of them! They raced out of the drawer, down the legs of the nightstand, and onto the floor. We screamed! Mrs. K. grabbed the nightstand, opened the front door, and flung the nightstand from the door clear out to the sidewalk, where it landed right on our trash pile.

"Here ya go, Dottie, come and get your goddamn nightstand!" she yelled before slamming the door shut. I rushed to the kitchen to get the can of bug killer that was on top of the refrigerator and ran back into the living room. When we were satisfied that we sprayed as many as we could, I swept them into a pile, onto a dustpan, and dumped them into the trashcan.

Grandmom set up the lamp on a rickety table in the dining room, and Mrs. K. directed me to wash the colander and put it in the cabinet underneath the kitchen sink. When I finished, I returned the baby stroller to the basement. We sat on the living room sofa and watched *Real People*, but I couldn't concentrate on it. All I could think of was poor Lorraine and the horrible life she was forced to lead in this indigent world of Southwest Philly.

Chapter Twenty-Two

Lorraine

The day of the Stonehurst Ball, I was so excited I thought I would die. The makeup artist and hair stylist came at four that afternoon to get me ready. When they were done, I looked like a movie star! After they left, one of the maids came up to help me get dressed. She walked into the little room at the back of the walk-in closet and wheeled out the gown on its dress form covered over with the sheet. Then she went and got the hoop for it. When she pulled off the sheet, I let out a big sigh. No matter how many times I saw it, I was still amazed.

I took off my robe and stood in my undies and strapless bra as she handed me a pair of black stockings. I slowly rolled them up my legs so I wouldn't snag them. Then she told me to step into the hoop, and she pulled it up and tied it around my waist. Then she carefully dropped the gown over me and smoothly zipped it up. I slipped into a pair of low-heeled black satin pumps she handed me and dabbed on a little bit of perfume from one of the vials on Daven's vanity. I found the jewelry for the gown in her jewelry armoire: a pair of sapphire-and-diamond earrings and a matching choker. The last things I put on were the long white gloves.

I went and stood in front of the full-length mirror to give myself a final look, and I was dazzled by what I saw. Lorraine Kowalski from the street corner was gone, and in her place stood a princess from a fairy tale! I wanted to cry but didn't in order to not ruin my makeup.

"You look lovely!" the maid said.

"Thank you," I replied, "and thank you for helping me get ready." I grabbed the small black evening bag that I already packed with my essentials and floated out the door. As I went down the staircase, the staff was there, all of them smiling at me. All except Consuelo, who muttered something under her breath and made the sign of the cross. I ignored her and refused to let her rain on my parade.

When I reached the bottom of the staircase, the maid who helped me get ready said, "Wait!" and grabbed a Polaroid camera that was sitting on a credenza. She snapped a few pictures of me at the bottom of the staircase and laid them on the credenza to dry.

Soon, we heard a car horn honk. I ran to the door, and a black limo was pulling up to the front of the house. Stuart popped out of the limo with a box in his hand. He looked so hot in his tuxedo. "You look beautiful," he said as I opened the door, and he gave me a small kiss. We walked into the foyer. He opened the box, and inside was a corsage of pink roses, which he slid onto my wrist. We posed for more pictures, then the staff said goodbye to us as we climbed into the limo and took off.

"I can't wait to see Stonehurst!" I said.

"Yes," he said, "I'm as excited as you are. The grounds are gorgeous, and Oliver and Claire Danford are good people." I had to force myself to stay still because I was bouncing around like a little kid. It didn't take long to get there. It was in Villanova, so it was very close. We pulled up to a big stone mansion behind a line of other limos and luxury cars. Stuart helped me out and told the limo driver to be back around midnight.

I placed my hand on his arm as we glided up the steps, through the double doors, and into a foyer that was even bigger than Arnant's. There was a butler standing there, and Stuart handed him a white card, which the butler read from and called out, "Mr. Stuart Darnley Worthington and Miss Daven Eleanor Barrett." The party was already in full swing, even though it had just started. A huge chandelier glowed down on the foyer, and an orchestra was set up at the end and was playing covers of popular songs, and there was a dance floor in front of the orchestra. At the other end of the foyer was a buffet, and there were tables placed here and there.

As we stood there admiring it all, a middle-aged couple approached us, and they were as decked out as we were. I assumed they were Oliver and Claire Danford, the hosts of the ball. Claire was wearing so many diamonds that they almost blinded me. They dripped off of every part of her. Her and Oliver both held what looked like martinis in these fancy little glasses with carved stems.

"Good evening," Oliver said, giving us both a big smile. "It's wonderful to see you both! Daven, congratulations on your acceptance to Vassar; your parents told us all about it. Thank you both for coming!"

"Thank you, and thank you for inviting us," I said. Me and Stuart moved on and mingled with the guests. He knew a lot of them, which was good, because I could let him do all the talking. A few people who knew Daven came up and talked to me, and I just played along. As far as I could tell, I was fooling them perfectly. A servant walked by us carrying a silver tray of champagne glasses, and me and Stuart grabbed two for ourselves. He told me it was called Veuve Cliquot. It was the first time I ever had champagne; I loved how the little bubbles exploded in my mouth!

I looked all around for Chandlee, and so much that I thought my head would snap off of my neck. Fortunately, I didn't see her. I relaxed and let myself enjoy the ball.

Daven

As Lorraine prepared herself for the Stonehurst ball, I also prepared myself for a big night out. I rimmed my eyes in black eyeliner and feathered my hair with a curling iron as I softly sang along to "Promises, Promises" by Naked Eyes, finishing the coiffure by clipping a feathered roach clip into my hair. From Lorraine's jewelry box, I selected a pair of long, dangling gold earrings that reached the middle of my neck.

I wore an outfit appropriate for that evening: a form-fitting, black-and-white striped shirt with princess sleeves, designer jeans, and black ankle boots. I shoved the requisite comb into my back pocket and slathered my lips with Kissing Potion. I draped a small, black cross-body bag on my shoulder as I ran downstairs to the front door.

The Dart pulled up, and I ran out to it and climbed in. A big gang was piled inside: Danny, Lynn, Nicky, Carol, Bobby, and I. On this outing, Bobby's other friend, Joey Mullen, and his girlfriend, Marianne Donohue, joined us. Eight of us in one car! The Dart had a bench seat in the front, which Bobby and I shared with Joey and Marianne. The girls mostly sat on the guys' laps to conserve space.

Our destination: the R and L dance in Collingdale. Collingdale was a little town in Delco on MacDade Boulevard, located near Southwest Philly. It was a few miles down the boulevard from the MacDade Mall and the MacDade House.

We arrived at the Collingdale Number Two Firehouse, walked upstairs to the second floor, and entered a large room resembling a banquet hall. A DJ was set up in a far corner, and the room was dark. The only light sources were a glittering disco ball and a traffic light that flashed intermittently. "I'll Tumble 4 Ya" by Culture Club played as patrons filed in. Soon, there were at least a hundred kids present.

This was a different crowd from the one I was accustomed to from my excursions to the MacDade House. The guys wore dress shirts and skinny ties, and the girls were replicas of Jennifer Beals from *Flashdance* with their cutoff sweatshirts, miniskirts, and high-heeled pumps. It was a different fashion style from the abundance of concert shirts and jeans favored by the burnouts who patronized the MacDade House.

"Burning Down the House" by The Talking Heads was the DJ's first song, and everyone danced wildly to it. Bobby grabbed my hand and danced with me, and I laughed. He rocked a painter's cap, sleeveless T-shirt, jeans, and checkerboard sneakers. We were two kids from a different neighborhood, but we still looked fabulous!

Despite all the balls and other social events I had attended, the R and L dance was the most thrilling. I loved dancing with these hip, fashionable Delco kids to Top Forty hits. Every minute with Bobby was a blast, not just at that dance, but anywhere I found myself with him. I tried not to think of the agonizing day that loomed on the horizon, the day I would have to end it.

Lorraine

I excused myself to use the bathroom, which was in a hallway behind the foyer. As soon as I came out, guess who I saw? Yep! What was it with that bitch? I was seeing her everywhere! Was she stalking me? I was surprised that I didn't hear the butler call out her name like he did with us. Then I realized that she probably got to the ball before we did, so of course, I wouldn't have heard her be announced.

"We meet again," she said, evil in her eyes. I had to admit she looked beautiful. She was wearing a strapless black gown with a long, full skirt that was made up of several tiers of tulle. She was also wearing black opera gloves, and her blonde hair was pinned up in a French twist. Long, dangly rhinestone earrings hung from her ears.

"Chandlee. I didn't know you were here," was all I could say. We were standing about six feet away from each other, a long credenza with a large mirror hanging over it at our side. The mirror reflected into the foyer. As far as I could tell from looking at the reflection, everyone was dancing. No one seemed to be looking at us.

"What do you want?" I asked. I was pissed now.

She gave a little laugh. "I should think that would be obvious." She leaned back against the credenza as if she was posing for a picture.

"Stuart dumped you fair and square," I snapped. "He couldn't stand you. You need to deal with that and move on. You're wasting your time."

Now, she stood upright, ready to do battle. "Give him up! I want him back! I know I screwed up. I can do better this time, and I will! All I need is for you to step out of the picture. You can easily do that."

I had enough. Enough of her stalking me at every event. Enough of her pressuring me to end it with Stuart. This blonde bitch was pushing me to my limit. "Now look here!" I said as I moved toward her so that

I could get closer to her and get up in her face. But I wasn't used to wearing a poufy gown with a hoop and crinolines! I tangled up my foot in my gown, lost my balance, and fell forward. I grabbed onto Chandlee for support. I didn't want to, but it was either that or I bust my face on the floor.

I aimed to grab her shoulders, but instead, my hands landed at the top of the bodice of her strapless gown. I grabbed hold of it – I had to to save myself!—and pulled it down with a loud tear of the fabric. To make matters even worse, I pulled down the black bustier she wore underneath it, and that ripped, too. She was completely topless, and I swear I did it by accident!

At first, what happened didn't register, and she was quiet. Then she looked down at herself and screamed. She flung one arm across her breasts and used her other hand to gather up her skirt, and she bolted into the foyer, toward the only way out available to her: the main door. But because she couldn't run properly using only one hand to hold up that huge, floofy skirt, she was forced to also use the other. This meant she had no coverage for her breasts!

As she hauled ass across the foyer, her breasts on display for all to see, the crowd parted like the Red Sea as they screamed, totally shocked. Claire fell back against Oliver with the back of her hand pressed against her forehead as her eyes fluttered and he fanned her with his hand. The men put their hands over the ladies' eyes. The band was in the middle of Bonnie Tyler's "Total Eclipse of the Heart" but stopped dead as soon as they saw Chandlee. Her date stumbled after her as they made a beeline for the door, Chandlee screaming the whole time. The horrified butler flung it open for them and slammed it shut as soon as they left.

The foyer was filled with loud voices; no one could believe what they just saw. The lead singer of the band was able to compose herself after a few minutes, and she resumed the song. As the song got rolling again, everyone simmered down and started dancing again.

Stuart rushed over to me. "My God, I didn't know Chandlee was here! Do you know what happened?" I told him about what just went down between me and her, and he laughed hysterically. "You sure put her in her place!" he said. He had tears in his eyes from laughing so hard. "I don't think we'll have any more problems with her in the future after tonight." We started dancing to the song, and it was as if the embarrassing Chandlee incident never happened because we and everyone else at the ball were so wrapped up in it and having a really good time.

Chapter Twenty-Three

Daven

We danced like crazy to the most popular songs of that summer. "Maniac," "Stand Back," and "Separate Ways" were just a few of the ones the DJ spun. After a string of high-energy songs, the familiar opening notes of Spandau Ballet's "True" filled the room, and couples paired up to slow dance. Bobby and I did, too. I loved the feel of his hands around my waist as we slowly swayed to the music. I closed my eyes and allowed it to carry me to a fantasy world with Bobby in love with me as the true me, Daven. I never wanted that night to end.

We stayed till close to midnight, and I reluctantly departed for Southwest Philly. I wished desperately that I had grown up in either Southwest Philly or in Delco, as insane as that sounds. That magical night at the R and L produced a yearning for that region's free and uncomplicated life that I still keenly feel all these years later.

Lorraine

After "Total Eclipse of the Heart" was over, a guy singer stepped up to the microphone and softly sang the opening notes to Spandau Ballet's "True." Ladies and men paired up, and so did me and Stuart. He waltzed me around a little; I tried my best to remember the waltz steps Daven taught me in boot camp. I saw a flash at the side of my face and looked up to see a photographer snapping our picture! "That's an *Inquirer* photographer," Stuart told me. Our picture was going to be in the paper! Cool!

The night ended around midnight with Oliver and Claire Danford coming up to the microphone and thanking us all for attending, and the crowd called out its thanks in return. The limo came for me and Stuart and took us back to Arnant. He kissed me goodnight at the door, and I let myself in and went right up to Daven's room. I took a rose from my corsage and pressed it into the pages of one of the heavy books on Daven's bookshelf. This would be my keepsake from this night.

There was a message from her on her answering machine letting me know she was okay and that she was going to the R and L dance in Collingdale that night. I couldn't wait for our next conversation when I would be able to tell her about the Chandlee incident. I knew she would think it would be hilarious!

v

The next weekend, me and Stuart saw another movie at the Ardmore. This time, it was *Return of the Jedi*. Even though it had been out all summer, there were still a lot of people there to see it. I overheard some of them saying they saw it multiple times. After the movie was over, even though I was stuffed full of popcorn and soda, we had dinner at Howard Johnson's in Villanova. I got a salad and soup so I wouldn't disappoint Stuart by not eating something.

I was lying on Daven's bed after I got home when the phone rang. I said, "Hello" in my best Daven voice, and a man's voice came over the line.

"Davvie, is that you? You sound different." I panicked, because of course, I didn't know who it was. I assumed it was Daven's dad and hoped I was right.

"It's me, Daddy," I said. And I must have been right because I wasn't corrected, and he kept on talking.

"I'm calling to let you know we're coming home early Tuesday afternoon. Clay will arrive sometime early that night. We're sending the limo up to JFK to get him."

"Okay, thanks for letting me know."

"We'll focus on Vassar when we come home and make the final arrangements. You leave a week from Sunday."

"Yes," I said. "I'm nervous, Daddy."

"Don't be, kiddo. We'll plan everything out and get you up to Poughkeepsie all good and in one piece. Going to let you go now. Love you and thinking of you."

Daven

I embarked on another trip to the MacDade Mall in the middle of August. Bobby and I were off to see *Return of the Jedi* at the cinema. This was by far the biggest movie of that summer. It had been playing at cinemas since Memorial Day weekend, and its popularity hadn't abated, as the crowds were still rather heavy almost three months after its release.

After the movie, we had delicious Sicilian pizza at a pizza joint in the mall called Italian Delight. The MacDade was a wonderful little mall, full of honest Delco types. I planned on visiting again at some point in the future when things had cooled off from this summer's activities.

We made our way back to Southwest Philly around nine that night. Bobby and I drove down Lindbergh Boulevard as "Winds of Change" by Jefferson Starship played on the radio. I leaned my head out the window as the wind blew my feathered hair in all directions. I felt more alive than I had ever felt in my life as we raced along this major Southwest Philly thoroughfare. These Southwest Philadelphians were blessed with tremendous *joie de vivre*. They lived life deeply, fully, and passionately. It was a life of no boundaries and limitless freedom, unlike mine. And there was so much freedom, all of it for the taking. They may have been lower-income people but were tremendously wealthy in this respect.

When the identity switch ended, I was going to miss this abundant freedom. All the advantages of my world, added together, couldn't equate to the freedom I found on the streets of Southwest Philly.

I put in my usual call to Lorraine that night and was pleasantly surprised to hear that she had seen *Jedi*, too.

Lorraine

Right on schedule, Daven's parents came back from the shore that Tuesday. They looked like your typical rich Main Line couple. Pepper was dressed in a Lily Pulitzer dress and a pair of leather sandals, and Clay Sr. wore a white polo shirt, white pants, and Docksiders.

I was on red alert for their arrival all morning and into the afternoon and was really nervous, too. They got there around one. "Angel!" Pepper cried when she saw me standing in the foyer waiting for them. She ran over to me and hugged me and kissed me on the cheek. She smelled like expensive perfume. Clay Sr. came up behind her and gave me a big hug.

"We have a little something for you," Pepper said as she pulled a box of salt-water taffy and a little flowered plastic bag from her big pocketbook. The bag contained a pair of earrings and a bracelet, both made from little seashells. "Thank you, it's beautiful!" I said. Of course, I couldn't keep any of that stuff. I'd have to put it aside for Daven. I helped them unload their luggage and put it in the foyer, and a few servants carried it all upstairs.

Clay Sr. put his arm around my shoulders as we walked to the morning room, a little room that they used for informal meals. "We missed you at Longport, Davvie. But we respected your need for quiet this summer, knowing you've had a busy past year. As I said on the phone, we're going to talk earnestly about Vassar now that we're together."

"Yes, please, Daddy," I said in my best Daven voice.

He gave me a funny look. "Your voice sounds different. Perhaps you're growing, changing into an adult before our eyes." He pulled me closer and kissed me on the side of the face. "You're going to go far in life, kiddo."

We sat at the table as Consuelo brought us lunch. She was giving me that look again. I thought she would put the tray down and then leave, but she didn't. Instead, she looked straight at Pepper and Clay Sr. and said, in Spanish, "*¡No es la misma! ¡No es la señorita Daven!*"

They both looked confused. "What are you talking about, Consuelo? Of course, Daven's the same. If she seems different, it's because she's grown up a lot this past year." Consuelo looked as if she was about to lose her mind. She made the sign of the cross and hurried out of the room. Me, on the other hand, I felt sick. I was so happy the identity switch was coming to an end in a week. Consuelo was making me more and more nervous. Hopefully, she would be the worst thing I'd have to deal with at Arnant. I picked up and bit into a tuna sandwich as Daven's parents told me all about their summer in Longport.

Chapter Twenty-Four

Lorraine

At seven that night, Clay Jr. came back from his summer in Europe. He jumped out of the limo as it rolled up to the front door of Arnant. He wore black Ray-Ban Wayfarer sunglasses, just like Tom Cruise wore in *Risky Business*; a pink polo shirt with a popped collar; Madras shorts; and Docksiders. I watched him as his dad hugged him and helped him unload his luggage from the limo. His dad and the limo driver lugged it all into the mansion as Clay Jr. strolled on in ahead of them, not even helping them.

He was one hundred percent different from all the guys I knew in Southwest Philly, not just because of the way he dressed and all his money, but because of his overall attitude, too. He acted as if he owned the world, which I'm sure was the outlook on life his money and social status gave him. He took off his sunglasses and smiled when he saw me.

"Davvie!" he cried, running straight at me and wrapping me in a bear hug. "How's my little sister been all summer?"

He had a mouth full of gleaming, perfectly white teeth, like something out of a toothpaste commercial. As he bent down to look at me, I looked up at him, trying my best to look happy to see him. The truth was, I had only known him for a few seconds, yet I already couldn't stand him. He looked like your typical rich, douchebag, preppy asshole. And I knew, as surely as the day was long, that he was going to cause trouble for me.

"I'm fine, Clay. How was Europe?" I asked.

"It was a blast! I'm sorry it's over. I can't wait for the pictures to be developed so that I can show you all the places I visited. You'll love them! He moved onto Pepper and gave her a hug, and she told him how happy she was that he was home.

We had a proper dinner in Arnant's big dining room. We even got all dressed up for the occasion. I wore a short-sleeved pink dress and pink flats with big pink flower ornaments on them from a shoe designer called Pappagallo. They were the nicest flats I'd ever worn. And I also wore Daven's gold add-a-bead necklace and a pair of tiny gold hoop earrings.

I didn't talk much; most of the conversation was about what Pepper and Clay Sr. did in Longport and all the things in Europe Clay Jr. saw. I thought I saw him stare strangely at me a few times, and again I thought of how happy I would be when the identity switch ended on Saturday.

Daven called right after dinner. "Your parents and brother all came home today," I told her.

"That's good. I can't wait to see them!" she said.

I lowered my voice for this next part: "Look, Daven, Saturday can't get here fast enough. Consuelo's been bugging out, and I thought your brother seemed kinda funny at dinner."

"Just hold on, Rainey. Saturday'll be here before you know it."

I sighed. "And I hope I make it out of Arnant alive."

v

The next morning, as I was walking downstairs to have breakfast, I walked past Clay Jr.'s bedroom. The door was open a crack. I peeked in and saw him sitting on the edge of his bed holding a little mirror on which was a line of coke. His other hand held a rolled-up dollar bill up to his nose, and he inhaled the coke in one quick snort. I stepped back, not surprised by what I saw.

Of course, he was a cokehead; I was willing to bet a lot of rich brats were. He certainly had enough money to buy it. Of course, if he ever got caught for it, he'd escape all punishment. Because I knew that rich people usually got away with stuff that poor people like me never would. Now, if I had gotten caught using coke, I'd have been locked up and the key thrown away.

After he was done snorting, he put all his coke stuff into a cigar box and stashed it in the bottom drawer of his nightstand. Something told me to make a mental note of this because it would be information I could use later. I remembered that cigar box and where it was kept. Then I moved on to breakfast.

Daven

Mrs. K. called out sick that Wednesday morning, suffering from summer flu. She spent the better part of the day in her bedroom watching TV while I prepared chicken soup and other foods needed for her convalescence and brought them up to her. I stayed in Lorraine's room listening to her boombox when I wasn't needed. "Take Me to Heart," the terrific new song from Quarterflash, was playing, and I was singing along to it when the door suddenly opened. Mrs. K. stood there looking flushed and disheveled in a robe, a flannel nightgown, and a pair of bedroom slippers.

"I gotta talk to you," she blurted as she strode into the room and plopped on the bed.

"Yeah, okay. What's up?"

"You've been acting funny lately. Like you're not you."

The cold perspiration of fear rolled down my back, and a lump rose in the back of my throat. "No, I'm the same I've always been."

"Your voice is weird. You act weird. I dunno, you seem like someone else."

I fought to keep my voice level. "I don't know what you're talking about."

She blinked at me a few times. "Maybe all this seems this way because I'm sick," she said, shaking her head and touching her stomach. "I feel too shitty to think about this anymore, and I gotta lay down. We'll talk about it again soon." She rose and padded off to her bedroom. As "Take Me to Heart" faded out, I trembled at the close call I had just had. I was now as eager as Lorraine was for the identity switch to end.

Lorraine

That afternoon, Clay Jr.'s friends Trevor and Josh stopped by to go swimming. I overheard their conversation from the far end of the terrace. They either didn't know I was sitting there or didn't care.

They were in the pool floating on chaise lounges and drinking Lowenbrau. "Fascination" by The Human League played from a boombox set up on a table.

"How was Europe?" the one called Trevor said.

Clay Jr. snorted. "Fuck, man, all I did was screw around. London, Madrid, Paris, Amsterdam, Geneva, Rome – a fuckfest and a party in every city. I met this one chick at a nightclub on my first night in Paris. She was smokin' hot and a model. I think her name was Celine or Clarisse or Collette or something like that. I banged her every night of my stay in Old Paree. When it was time for me to move on to the next venue, she bawled her eyes out and told me she had fallen in love with me and didn't want me to go. I gave her my address and digits and promised to keep in touch. I think I even told her I would bring her here for Christmas."

The one called Josh spit out the gulp of Lowenbrau he just took. "Shit, man, you gave her your contact info? And you said you're gonna bring her here for Christmas? Why'd you do that?"

Clay Jr. let out a big laugh. "Relax, dude, it was a fake address and a fake phone number, and I used a fake name, too. I'm obviously not going to bring her here, either. That little piece is never going to find me. She gave me one of her necklaces as a reminder of her. I gave it to a hooker in Amsterdam." Laughs and high-fives all around followed, and I was so disgusted by them. They were the scummiest people I'd ever met, scummier than even the most low-class, white-trash family in my neighborhood. And Clay Jr. was the ringleader of it all.

And I felt sorry for this French girl, whoever she was. Thanks to this asshole, she was going to have trust issues with guys for the rest of her life.

I spent the rest of the day in Daven's room watching MTV and reading her stack of *Seventeen*s. With Clay Jr. creeping around, I didn't feel safe wandering around the mansion. I was feeling really bugged out. I kept getting a bad feeling about him that wouldn't go away, and I prayed to God that Saturday would get here fast. I put my mind back on MTV as the video for the Billy Joel song "Uptown Girl" came on. Right away, I recognized that the girl in the video was Christie Brinkley, the model.

Daven

Bobby and I stood on the 67th Street bridge that night looking at the GE building as it loomed over us. "One on One" by Hall and Oates played from a passing car's stereo. "Joey Mullen's having a party in his basement; wanna go?" he asked me. "Sure," I said. We walked over the crosswalk to the other side of the tracks and then to a back alley behind the row homes on Glenmore Avenue. We stopped at the back door of one of the houses, and Bobby knocked. The door was opened by Joey Mullen, and out wafted the scents of cigarette smoke and marijuana.

"Glad youse could make it!" he cried out. His girlfriend Marianne Donohue hovered behind him, and behind her were a bunch of kids I didn't know seated on a sofa and chairs. In the middle of the gathering was an Igloo cooler filled with ice and cans of Budweiser. On a table next to it stood bottles of Southern Comfort, Jack Daniels, and Boone's Farm Strawberry Hill. The boombox played "Jeopardy" by Greg Kihn. Joey ushered us into the basement, and we sat on folding metal chairs. Bobby reached forward, grabbed two cans of Bud from the cooler, and handed me one. I hated beer, but in my role as Lorraine, I had no choice but to drink it.

A joint passed my way, but I declined it. Bobby looked strangely at me and passed it on to Danny, who took a hit and passed it on to Lynn. As the joint made its way around, I noticed, for the first time, the two girls sitting across from me. I should add that they were staring at me, and not in a very friendly way. They both wore heavy black eyeliner that reduced their eyes to slits, and they sported identical feathered hairstyles with roach clips in them.

"Hi!" I chirped. "My name's Lorraine. Do youse live around here?" I silently praised myself for remembering to use the working-class-Philadelphia vernacular's second-person plural of that pronoun.

"We're Joanne and Terri. We live at 65th and Wheeler."

"Oh, I'm on Bonnaffon Street. We live close to each other!" But Joanne and Terri didn't seem impressed and rolled their eyes. I said nothing more to them and began talking to Bobby, Nicky, and Carol. Eventually, I began to feel nauseous from the mixture of beer, cigarette smoke, marijuana, and bad vibes, and I made haste for the back alley.

As I stood taking breaths of fresh air and enjoying the balmy night breeze, I heard footsteps. I turned to see Joanne and Terri descending upon me, closely crowding me in.

My stomach knotted in fear.

"You ain't right," Joanne said.

"What are you talking about?" I said.

"The way you were acting back there, all prissy and shit," Terri answered. "You let that joint pass you by, and I could tell you were struggling to get that beer down your throat. I didn't see you smoking no cigarettes, either."

"We think you're full of shit," Joanne spat, and I jumped back at this accusation.

"I don't know what youse are talking about, but – "

Terri cut me off. "You ain't from around here, and we can tell. We call bullshit on you living on Bonnaffon. As a matter of fact, we don't think you're from Southwest at all. You're probably some snooty bitch from Delco who goes to Prendie or one of those fancy schools out that way. You're on the wrong turf."

I was taken aback and at a loss for words. Was I going to be assaulted now? Because it seemed to be the next logical step for these two. Therefore, it was no surprise when Joanne grabbed the front of my shirt and growled into my face, "We don't wanna see you around here again, you dig? We don't need your kind here. Now get the fuck back to your party, and when it's over, you get the fuck back to where you came from." She released me, and she and Terri turned and walked down the alley and into the night, not bothering to return to the party. I could hold back my tears no longer and began to cry profusely.

Chapter Twenty-Five

Lorraine

Things were icky the next day, too. I had to put up with Clay Jr. staring strangely at me all during breakfast. I was too afraid he'd start grilling me afterward, so I hopped on Daven's bike and took another tour of the Main Line just to get myself out of the house and away from him. As I was leaving, I heard him talking in Spanish to Consuelo. I didn't have to ask to know that the conversation was about me!

I came back to Arnant a few hours later, wishing I could have stayed out all day but knowing it wasn't realistic to do that. I put Daven's bike back in the shed and moved as fast as I could up to her bedroom. I decided I was going to hole up there for the next two days until Saturday rolled around and the identity switch would be over.

As I was walking down the hallway toward her room, I heard a noise coming from inside it. I walked in and found Clay Jr. sitting on Daven's bed. I almost threw up when I saw what he was holding: my school ID! Oh, my God, I realized I left it right on the nightstand that morning to remind myself that I would be back to my normal self in two days, and I forgot to put it back in its hiding place! Oh, God, Daven was gonna kill me!

We stared at each other like two deer in the headlights. He looked at my ID for a second or two and then looked back at me. Then he said, "I knew something was up. I wondered why Daven seemed different. Turns out she wasn't Daven at all. Lorraine Kowalski, you have a lot of explaining to do. You can start by telling me where my sister is."

v

Scared doesn't even begin to describe the way I was feeling about Clay Jr. finding my school ID. I knew at that minute that me and Daven had to end our game like right now. There was no way we could keep pulling it off now that the cat was out of the bag, so I poured out the whole story. All of it.

"You dumb bitch," he snarled when I was finished. "Did you and Daven really think you could get away with this? What the hell possessed you both to do this? Even if it was her idea, you still played along with it.

"You tell me Daven's been slumming at your shithole house in Southwest Philly pretending to be you. Where the fuck is that? I can figure it out geographically, but where exactly is it?" I started to tell him before he cut me off. "I don't give a fuck where it is, actually. I'm incensed that this happened. Do you know how powerful my family is? Or who my father is? We'll sue you for this. We can afford to hire the best lawyers to do it, too. We'll end you and your entire white-trash family."

I felt overwhelmed and started to cry. I knew his threats were real, too, and not bullshit. What were me and Daven going to do? Then he dropped his ax:

"My parents and I are paying a visit tonight to one of my advisors, who has a house in Bryn Mawr. We need to see her to discuss my internship this year. You're not expected to come, and that's just as well, because I want to spend that time thinking long and hard about how I'm going to bust you."

He walked over to the bedroom door and was about to leave, but then he turned around and said, "And if you and my sister switch back to your normal selves while I'm gone, I'll bust you anyway – and her, too, because I'm hugely pissed off at her for doing this. But I'll save most of my vitriol for you because I hate your kind; you low-class city people make me sick. I'll rake you over the coals good, you little street punk, so be prepared."

v

I waited on pins and needles for Daven's call that night. I was so scared I was ready to throw up. When the phone rang around seven, about half an hour after Clay and his parents left, I almost jumped out of my skin, it startled me so bad.

I picked it up without even saying hello, knowing that it was her. "Daven, listen to me, we have to end it now."

I could tell she was scared by the way her voice cracked. "Why? What's happened?"

I gave her a fast instant replay of Clay Jr.'s discovery and him busting me. Then we both started to cry.

"I'm sorry!" Daven blubbered. "This is all my fault! I should have listened to you and never insisted that we switch identities! I know we were going to end it in only two more days, on Saturday, but we have to end it now!"

"Go back to my house, grab whatever stuff of yours you have there, get in a taxi, and come back here to Arnant," I ordered. "Never mind Clay's threat to bust both of us if we do the switcheroo when he's gone; as you just said, we have to end this now. Even if you remember how to take public, don't do it; it won't get you here in time. As soon as you get here, we'll do the switcheroo, and I'll scram away as fast as I can and take public back to Southwest Philly. Act fast because your brother and parents just went out, and you want to get here before they come back."

"Yes. I'll get moving now." Without even saying goodbye, she hung up, leaving me sitting on the floor curled in a ball and crying my eyes out real bad.

Daven

> As soon as I hung up with Lorraine, I bolted back to her house, my heart beating a mile a minute. I planned to walk into the house as calmly as possible, go up to Lorraine's room, put my things in her tote bag, and nonchalantly tell Mrs. K I would listen to metal albums at Bobby's house.

When I got there, I waited until my breathing slowed before entering. Grandmom must have been in her room because I didn't see her. Mrs. K. was watching *The People's Court* in the living room. Lying next to her was the past Sunday's edition of the *Philadelphia Inquirer*, folded open to the Society section, and she was staring at it. On the first page was an article about the Stonehurst ball, and to my surprised delight, there was Lorraine. She was smiling from ear to ear as she and Stuart Worthington waltzed into the picture frame, and she looked beautiful in my gown! I was elated! It was exactly the kind of experience I wanted her to have as me!

But my elation evaporated into fear when Mrs. K. turned to face me, giving me a cold death stare that cut right into the center of my soul. She shut off the TV, picked up the newspaper, and studied the picture before her for a few seconds. It seemed an eternity before she spoke.

"Lorraine, I wondered why you seemed so different these past few months. I thought maybe it was because you just graduated from high school and were going through a lot of stuff because of the big change in your life. That's why I talked to you about it a little while back when I was sick. But I didn't bring it up again because I thought it was best to let you go through whatever transition you were making toward adulthood. But here I see you at some fancy ball. How did you manage to sneak off to a ball? And where did you get this gown?

"Or are you not Lorraine at all? The name here says Daven Barrett. In fact, I'll read you the whole caption: 'Miss Daven Barrett and Mr. Stuart Worthington waltz the night away at the summer ball hosted by Mr. and Mrs. Oliver Danford at the Stonehurst estate in Villanova.' But I know that's my daughter in the picture. Daven Barrett, you have a lot of explaining to do. You can start by telling me where my daughter is."

Chapter Twenty-Six

Lorraine

I waited in the foyer for Daven, hoping and praying that she would get there before her parents and brother did so that we could switch back to our normal selves, and I could split out of there. I wasn't too worried about how I would get home. I could walk the mile or so to the Haverford train station and get back to Southwest Philly from there; it wasn't a big deal. I held Daven's tote bag and her pocketbook, both of which were filled with my stuff, which I would put into my tote bag and pocketbook that she was bringing with her. I sat in one of the chairs, waiting for a taxi to pull up at any moment and Daven to hop out.

Through one of the windows, I saw the headlights of an oncoming car. It stopped at the portico, and I heard one of the car's doors open and someone get out. I almost cried because I was so relieved that Daven was finally there. I ran to the door and flung it open to find my mother standing there. Not Pepper Barrett, but my real mother, Sandra Kowalski, with Daven by her side.

Daven

Mrs. K. had busted me good when she saw Lorraine's picture in the paper. I had no choice but to tell her the whole story of the identity switch; she had been livid. After I had finished, she had said, "All right, now take me to this fancy-schmancy place you live at and take me to my daughter. I'm gonna get to the bottom of this bullshit right now."

There I was, standing at the door of my own home, looking like the sorriest person in the world. Mrs. K. looked incredulous, enraged, and confused all at once. She grabbed me by the arm and dragged me into the foyer. I rushed to stand by Lorraine. Whatever happened next, we were going to face it together.

"Jesus Christ, youse do look identical," Mrs. K. exclaimed, taking us both in with one glance. "And Daven tells me it was her idea for you to switch identities."

"Don't put all the blame on her," Lorraine said. "It's half my fault, too."

Mrs. K. sneered at Lorraine and turned away. She walked around the foyer, giving it a good look. "Well, shit, here I am in rich man's country. Who'da thought? I feel like I'm in *High Society*. That's an old Grace Kelly movie; I saw it when I was in high school. She played a rich Main Line girl, just like Daven here. Lordy, lordy. What are the odds of people like you and me, Lorraine, winding up in a place like this? Is this happening?"

She sounded facetious but wasn't. Soon, my parents and Clay would return from his advisor's home, and the drama would amplify. I felt sick, and the greenish cast on Lorraine's face told me she felt the same.

Mrs. K opened her mouth to speak but was interrupted by the sound of my parents' car pulling up to the house. A few seconds later, they entered, with Clay trailing behind them. They struggled to process what they were seeing, incredulous not only by the extreme similarities between Lorraine and me but also by the sight of Mrs. K. and her working-class appearance.

"Whaaat...?" Daddy gasped, as Mummy clutched his arm, trying not to collapse. I had never seen her so close to fainting. Clay's mouth opened and closed noiselessly several times. In all probability, he planned to do what Lorraine had told me: rat us out, bust us good, and revel in our downfall. Now that Mummy and Daddy had discovered the truth unaided by him, he had been thwarted.

He would have had no qualms about busting me along with Lorraine. I loved my brother but would have been the first to admit he was a snake who wouldn't have hesitated to stoop that low.

Mrs. K. explained the situation and took the wind out of Clay's sails in one fell swoop. "Yeah, my name's Sandy Kowalski, and this," she poked Lorraine, "is my daughter Lorraine. Our identical-looking daughters switched identities at the beginning of the summer. Until today, I thought your daughter was mine, and apparently vice versa for you."

All hell broke loose. She, Mummy, and Daddy began a shouting match while Lorraine and I protectively clung to each other. Their shouts echoed throughout the foyer as the argument became increasingly heated, and Lorraine and I separated them.

"How could this have happened?" Mummy cried, looking straight at Lorraine.

"Hey, your kid's at fault, too!" Mrs. K. yelled back.

"Mom and Dad, call the police! Have them arrested and sue the pants off them!" Clay bellowed, determined to play a role of some kind in my and Lorraine's downfall.

"Clay, maybe we should," Mummy said to Daddy as they simmered. Daddy straightened the lapels on his jacket and said, "Maybe that's not a bad idea. We've had an interloper in our midst for the past two months. She's had an intimate look at our family and everything in it. Who's to say she won't drag us through the mud?"

"Yeah, well, I could sue the pants off of youse, too!" Mrs. K. thundered. "I had an interloper in my house for two months, too!"

A deafening pall hung, and I began to fear for Mrs. K. I didn't doubt that she had had to battle all kinds of monsters throughout her life, but my parents had the potential to be the worst of them. It was one thing for her to defend herself in a street fight or against an abusive husband, but how would she defend herself against a wealthy, powerful Main Line family that could use all its money and influence to destroy her, being as penniless and as powerless as she was?

Fear flitted across her face as she realized the folly of her words and the reality of her situation. She looked like a mouse that had been spotted by a cat and wanted nothing more than to find a corner to run into.

Clay folded his arms across his chest and grimed smugly as the winds blew in his favor. But Lorraine—wonderful, street-smart

Lorraine—came to the rescue and said, "Well, Mr. and Mrs. Barrett, you should know that your son has a nice coke habit."

Lorraine

I hadn't learned to survive Southwest Philly's mean streets without keeping an ace up my sleeve, and now was the time to pull it out. I knew the Barretts were going to move in for the kill on me and Mom, so I told them about Clay Jr.'s little problem to get us out of that tight spot.

Clay Jr. looked startled, then laughed an evil laugh. "Really, Lorraine Kowalski? Are you really going to do this? You've already been proven to be a liar; why should anyone believe anything you say?"

Without saying a word, I ran up the staircase to Clay Jr.'s room. I opened the bottom drawer of his nightstand, hoping his coke kit would be there, and it was. I grabbed it and ran back down to the foyer.

"Here you are, Mr. and Mrs. Barrett," I said, handing the kit to Clay Sr. He flipped open the lid of the cigar box, and his face turned black when he saw what was in there.

"This is yours?" he asked Clay Jr., who, for once, had nothing to say. Pepper snatched the box away from him to give it a good look, and then Daven and Mom leaned toward it to do likewise. Now the hot topic switched from me and Daven to Clay Jr. as we all stared at him. We all waited for him to talk, but he just gave a blank look.

It was Clay Sr. who spoke up. "Clay, I'm calling your advisor tomorrow and telling her you won't be taking that internship. That's because you'll be spending the school year in rehab. When it's over, you can resume your studies at Cornell and graduate the following year."

"You can't do that!" Clay Jr. cried.

"Oh, yes, we can!" Pepper snapped.

"This is bullshit!" he yelled. Then he turned to look at me. "This is all your fault!" he snarled. "You little hood rat! I'm going to get you for this!"

"Who you callin' a hood rat?" Mom yelled at him, her courage coming back to her. "You're the junkie. Fess up to it!"

"Ah, shut the fuck up, you trashy bitch!" Clay Jr. screamed at her. It was a huge, fatal mistake, because that's when Mom decked him square in the face. He screamed like a girl as he fell backwards. Right away, all hell broke loose for a second time as Clay Sr. and Pepper began another screaming match with Mom, who stood her ground pretty good against them. She, like me, had lived through a lot of street fights with people far worse than these two. Me and Daven clung to each other, protecting each other, as the second battle of the parents played out. There was a lot of pushing and shoving, and when it simmered down, Clay Sr.'s glasses were dangling off of one ear.

Clay Jr. was cowering in a corner of the foyer the whole time. Clay Sr. turned to look at him and yelled, "Clay, go to your room. We'll talk later." Clay Jr. bolted up the staircase and ran away like the little bitch he was. Clay Sr. straightened his glasses and took one look at me and Daven clutched together. "My God, what the hell are you wearing?" he asked. He was talking to Daven, who was wearing an Ozzy concert shirt, a pair of cutoff denim shorts, bunched tube socks, and high-top Nike sneakers. All my clothes, of course.

Pepper took a look at Daven, too, and cried, "Jesus Christ! Get those filthy rags off you!" Then she turned to look at me. "And you," she snarled, "get out of that shirt and those shorts. That's a Lilly Pulitzer short set that costs more than your mother makes in a day." Mom looked as if she wanted to say something about that, but she kept her mouth shut.

"Both of you go upstairs, get changed, and come back down. This charade is officially over now," Pepper said. I grabbed Daven by the hand and took her up the staircase with me. We were both crying.

Chapter Twenty-Seven

Daven

When we reached my room, I went into the bathroom to get undressed as Lorraine did in the bedroom. We traded clothes through the cracked-open bathroom door. In a few minutes, we were dressed as our usual selves. We emptied the contents of our tote bags and handbags, which we had remembered to carry with us after the melee, onto my bed, and took back our belongings. I haphazardly threw my belongings into a pile to be put away later. We also returned our driver's licenses and handbags and refilled them with their original contents. We departed my bedroom, Lorraine carrying her tote bag filled with her belongings, and walked back down the staircase like two prisoners being led to their execution. Mummy, Daddy, and Mrs. K. talked quietly and much more civilly.

"We'll be going now," Mrs. K. said when Lorraine reached her side. "I'm sorry, Mr. and Mrs. Barrett, for losing my temper, and I'm also sorry for the inconvenience and embarrassment this has caused youse. I'll make sure my daughter doesn't bother youse again, and youse won't hear from any of us, either."

At those words, a lump rose in my throat. Here was the most solid friendship I had ever made being smashed to pieces, the pronouncement of it uttered in a Southwest Philly accent. Southwest Philly had started our friendship and was ending it, too. I glanced at Lorraine and saw she felt the same way I did. I wanted to run to her, hold her close, and never let her go.

"Thank you, Mrs. Kowalski, for your discretion," Daddy said. "I don't know what got into our girls to make them do this. It looks as if Daven was acting out, and there was no need for her to do that. We give her everything any young girl could want. This is very embarrassing for us, and we're sorry. We promise not to pursue legal action." *You give me everything except total freedom and absolute control over my life,* I thought bitterly.

"And thank you," Mrs. K. replied. "Sorry things got out of hand a minute ago. We won't pursue any legal action, either." She pulled her car keys out of her tattered purse and said to Lorraine, as she grabbed her arm, "All right, let's go. The game is up." I watched them cross the foyer to the door with a heart that felt like a stone. My mother grabbed my arm the same way, her grip like a vice.

I couldn't let it happen. I couldn't let Lorraine glide out of my life. I needed her more than all the debutante balls, fancy cars, designer clothes, and country clubs in the world. She couldn't be spirited off; she just couldn't! Before I could choke it back, a ragged word jumped out of my throat: "Lorraine!" As it echoed throughout the foyer, I shook free of my mother's grasp and ran to her.

"Daven!" she cried back, shaking free of her mother. We ran and enfolded each other in a bear hug, never wanting to let go, and sobbed loudly.

"Best friends forever!" she cried, as our parents approached us and pulled us apart.

"Best friends forever!" I cried back as Mrs. K. hustled Lorraine out of my home and to their dilapidated car. I struggled for a minute against my parents' firm grip before breaking free and running feebly out of the house and after Lorraine and her mother as their car moved down the driveway. I collapsed in a heap on the gravel and sobbed uncontrollably as it turned onto the road and vanished into the night. I could barely hear my parents' footsteps crunching as they ran behind me and gathered me up.

Despite all I had endured that night, the most mundane detail tore me apart: the Lilly Pulitzer short set I was wearing, which Lorraine had been wearing twenty minutes earlier. The short set that cost more than Mrs. K. made in a day.

Lorraine

I don't know how I survived that ride home. Mom screamed at me the whole time, from the time we left Arnant until the time we pulled up in front of our house. A good forty-five minutes of screaming. She dragged me out of the car and into the house. Grandmom was waiting for us, sitting on the sofa and watching *Too Close for Comfort*.

Mom cracked me across the face, and good. "So, that's what you've been doing all summer! Passing yourself off as some rich mucky-muck! Did you have fun? How many balls and country clubs did you go to?" I couldn't talk, couldn't defend myself in any way. I fell onto the sofa and cried. I was surprised I had any tears left at this point.

"Sandy, what the hell's going on? Youse just raced outta here without saying nothing to me," Grandmom said. Mom plopped next to her on the sofa, positioning herself between me and Grandmom. All three of us on the sofa, each of us experiencing different emotions. She launched into the story of me and Daven's identity switch. Grandmom turned off the TV so she could hear Mom better, and as Mom talked, it was so quiet that the only sound I could hear was the whirring noise of Grandmom's oxygen tank.

When Mom was done talking, Grandmom screamed, "Jesus Christ!" She jumped up and reached for the oxygen tank. It looked like she wanted to throw it at me, but then she thought twice and dropped her hand. "This is unfuckingbelievable!" she cried.

"Mom, sit down. All this excitement isn't good for you." Grandmom sat down and rested her head on her hand as she took a few deep breaths. Mom said to me, "Do you see what you did to your grandmother? You almost fucking killed her. Only the three of us will know about this. Don't tell Paulie, Dierdre, or anyone else in the family, and for Christ's sake, don't tell any of your friends, either. This is beyond fucking embarrassing. Lorraine, get up to your room. Tomorrow, we're gonna talk about what you'll do when the summer's over. I want you to apply at Katharine Gibbs and do something useful with your life. And you're not to have any contact with Daven. It's a fucking miracle that her parents didn't sue us. Jesus Christ!"

I walked up to my room, changed into pajamas, and flopped into bed. I was just about to fall asleep when I thought about Stuart. I couldn't leave him hanging. I would have to call him the next day and explain everything. The thought of doing that was even worse than what I just lived through that night. I hoped that death would take me before I woke up the next morning.

Daven

The next thing I remembered, I was sitting in my room in my pajamas. I assumed Mummy had led me up there and changed me. I sat like a zombie, waiting to shed tears that wouldn't come. Daddy knocked on the door, and Mummy called for him to enter. They both looked gravely at me, as much at a loss for words as I was.

Daddy spoke in a voice full of suppressed anger. "We gave you a summer of freedom. The whole house was yours. We knew we had kept you on too tight a tether, so for once in your life, we left you to your own devices. And you violated our trust by pulling off this charade!" He paced back and forth across my bedroom, then turned to look at me. "Your mother and I thought something was off about you right after we returned from Longport. You didn't seem like yourself. At times, you seemed like a different person altogether. Well, now we know why! It's because you *were* a different person altogether!" I sagged against Mummy and quietly sobbed.

Daddy continued to pace my bedroom, his face every shade of red. "We were going to confront you about the change, but we put it down to the stress of starting college. We chose to wait until you were established at Vassar before we questioned you. But Mrs. Kowalski let the cat out of the bag by showing up tonight. If not for her, the charade would still be in full swing.

"You're to have nothing to do with those people again, do you hear me? They're trash. That girl is trash, her mother is trash, and her family is trash. Your mother and I don't want you consorting with trash!"

Daddy's reviling of Lorraine snapped me out of my stupor. "Lorraine's not trash! She's a good person! She's the only true friend I've ever had! Of course, you hate her. You hate anyone who's not rich, and you especially hate the working poor. Lorraine may be some impoverished street kid from Southwest Philly, but she has a heart of gold. Do you know how easy it would have been for her to keep walking the night I got lost there? She had nothing to gain from helping me. Without her, I could have ended badly in a neighborhood like that. But she was there, and she protected me. You might want to be mindful of that," I added bitterly.

This mollified Mummy and Daddy. "She's right, Clay," Mummy said quietly. "I know we're furious with what Daven and Lorraine have done, but if it weren't for Lorraine, who knows what would have happened to Daven? Let's remember that and put this behind us. It will stay in the family, and we'll ensure Clay keeps it to himself, too."

Perhaps her words had the correct effect on Daddy because he had nothing more to say. They kissed me goodnight, turned out my light, and departed my room, shutting the door behind them.

I thought of Bobby. I would have to call him the next day and explain everything. The thought of doing that was a hundred times worse than I had lived through that night. To calm myself, I tuned my clock radio to a soft-rock station and set the timer to shut off in an hour. "Human Nature" by Michael Jackson was the last song I heard before I slid into an uneasy sleep.

Chapter Twenty-Eight

Lorraine

Mom headed off to work early the next morning, and Grandmom stayed in her room. I didn't see either of them when I woke up. Knowing what I had to do, I picked up the phone and dialed Stuart's number. Fortunately, he, and not his family or staff, answered the phone.

"Stuart, I have to talk to you," I said, without even saying hello first, holding back my tears. I dropped my Main Line accent and talked in my normal voice, as I had nothing to lose now. This was the moment I dreaded.

"What's on your mind, pumpkin? And why all of a sudden do you sound different?"

I didn't even answer that; it didn't matter anymore what I sounded like. As difficult as it was, I had to end it now. Not only would I probably not get a chance to call him again, but the sooner I ended it, the better it would be all the way around. Also, I needed to talk to him without Mom or Grandmom being around.

"Are you okay?" he asked.

"Yes – no," I stuttered. Oh God, I thought, please give me the strength to get through this. "Stuart, I have to tell you something: I'm not who you think I am."

"What do you mean?" he asked.

"I – me – I'm not Daven Barrett. My real name is Lorraine Kowalski." And out it all came, all of it, all the sticky details. Finally, I was done. As painful as it was, it was a relief to get it all off my chest.

When he was able to talk, he said, "You and Daven concocted this deception on a lark?"

"Yeah," I blurted. "It was her idea, actually. But please don't put all your anger on her. I agreed to go along with it, so you should blame us fifty-fifty."

He gave a funny little laugh. "Was it all a lie? All the times we spent together? All the times we said we loved each other? Was it all a lie, all a part of the deception?"

"No!" I cried, the tears running down my face. "It wasn't a lie! I love you, Stuart! You don't know how much! When me and Daven agreed to do this, I never thought I'd get involved with anyone, and certainly not with someone as fabulous as you are. You're my everything!" I started crying very hard now. I knew he hated me; who could blame him? I had strung him along, and he had, in good faith, started a relationship with me. I couldn't blame him for the way he felt.

"Then it's over," he said, in a hollow voice. "I don't know who you are, and I don't trust you. I thought you were Daven Barrett, and I've come to find out you were someone different all along. Please tell me how I'm ever going to trust you again."

"I know," I said in a small voice. "You have every right not to." My heart felt like it was going to burst out of my chest. It was honestly the worst feeling I had ever felt in my life, and that was really saying something.

We didn't talk; neither of us knew what to say. Then he spoke up: "I won't tell anyone about this. I refuse to create embarrassment for Daven, you, or me. We're over now. If people ask why I split up with Daven, I'll say we had differences and leave it at that. Is there anything else you'd like to say?" he asked. He sounded as if he was going to cry.

"Look," I said, "I have to ask. Is the fact that I'm from the wrong side of the tracks any part of the reason you're dumping me?"

He gave a sharp laugh; I could tell he was pissed. "Yeah. Think that if it makes you feel better." Then he hung up. It was the last time we would ever talk.

Daven

Consuelo brought breakfast to my room the next morning on Mummy and Daddy's instructions. As soon as she departed, I called Bobby. I wanted to die, but I had to get it over with.

"Bobby, we have to talk," I said as soon as he picked up, in my normal Main Line voice. There was no longer any point in maintaining the façade.

"What's on your mind, sugar? And why do you sound different?" he asked. I felt ill, as the moment I had dreaded was at last at hand. Oh, God, how was I going to make it through this? I took several deep gulps of air and braced myself for the worst. "Are you okay?" he asked.

"Bobby, I'm not who you think I am. I'm not Lorraine Kowalski. My real name is Daven Barrett." The story of the identity switch poured out of me in slow, agonizing waves. I sagged, heaving in my chair at its conclusion.

"Are you serious?" he croaked.

"Yes!" I sobbed. "It was my idea. I thought it would be fun for Lorraine and me to switch identities. She didn't want to do it, Bobby. I swear to you, she didn't. I talked her into it, so if you want to blame someone, blame me!"

I could tell he was holding back tears. "Was it all bullshit, then? Us telling each other how much we loved each other? Was our relationship part of your trick?"

"No!" I cried. "Bobby, I never meant to get involved with anybody! But when I first saw you, I had to have you. You're like no one I've ever met! When I was with you, for the first time in my life, I felt alive!"

"Seriously?" he said scornfully. "I'm better than all those rich fucking assholes you've spent all your life around?"

"Yes! Bobby, you don't know the terrific person you are! You showed me that life could be exciting, fulfilling, and totally without limits. No one has ever shown me that."

He sighed. "Yeah, I wanna believe everything you're telling me; you don't know how fucking bad, either. But you're a huge fucking liar!"

"I'm sorry! I'm so sorry!" I sobbed. "You must hate me so much, but please don't drag Lorraine's name through the mud. I beg you to keep this incident to yourself. Lorraine doesn't deserve to be viciously gossiped about. I love her as if she were my sister." I waited for his response, fearing that he would spitefully refuse to keep the secret and blab it to everyone. I didn't care about myself at that juncture; I deserved what I was getting. All I wanted was his promise not to hurt Lorraine.

"Yeah, all right," he said. "I'll keep this shit to myself. As for you, we're history. Thanks for the memories." He slammed the phone down. That was the last conversation we would have.

Lorraine

The next afternoon, I snuck up to the payphone across the street from the library and called Daven. I could tell she was crying.

"I'm so sorry, Lorraine," she cried. "It was all my fault! I should have listened to you, but I wanted a break from my life and thought we could be each other just for the summer. I'm sorry!"

I was crying, too. "No, it's my fault, too. I could have walked away from it but didn't."

"I broke up with Bobby. I hurt him so badly; it was awful. Did you break up with Stuart?"

"Yeah, and I felt like shit about my breakup, too." I got quiet for a few seconds, then I asked, "What's gonna happen to Clay? Are your parents really gonna send him to rehab?"

"Yes, they are, to a facility in Chester County. I forget its name."

"Should we tell our friends the truth, like we told our boyfriends? My mom doesn't want me to, but maybe I should."

"No, it would be best if we left things status quo. In other words, don't tell them. We had to tell Bobby and Stuart, as they were our boyfriends. They've been sworn to secrecy, but we can't be sure our friends will be as discreet and honorable if we tell them the truth. There will be nothing to be gained by it. No, let's not tell our friends. It's dishonest, but telling the truth would cause too many problems."

We just cried for a minute, then she was able to talk again. "Lorraine, I love you. I've never had a real best friend before, and you're the best best friend anyone could ask for."

"You're my best friend, too," I cried.

"We might never see or hear from each other again. My parents will trace all my calls from now on, so I won't be able to call you anymore, nor should you call me. Don't write to me, either, because they'll check my mail, too."

It killed me to hear this. Daven was the best thing in my life. She was the only person in my life who didn't criticize or judge me. She was a best friend sent straight down from heaven. And now I could never talk to her again.

"What will you do now?" I asked.

"My parents and I are driving to Vassar tomorrow," she said. "It's freshman move-in day, and then there will be a week of orientation before next Monday's first day of class. After that, I won't be back at Arnant until Christmas break. Not that we'll be able to see each other."

"I'll miss you," I said. "I'll think about you every day."

"I'll miss you and think about you every day, too. Lorraine, I have to go. Thank you for a good summer, even if we did get busted horribly. Always remember you have a best friend on the Main Line."

The line went dead, and I hung up the phone. I stood and cried some more, and I couldn't move. A car driving down The Avenue was playing "King of Pain" by The Police. It's such a sad, desolate song, and it perfectly fit the way I was feeling.

Chapter Twenty-Nine

Daven

All that day and the next were consumed with packing me up for the drive to Vassar. Mummy and Daddy said very little to me, for which I was grateful, as I struggled to get my head straight from the recent drama. I made so many trips from my bedroom, down to the U-Haul van parked in the driveway, and back that I was exhausted by the time evening rolled around. By early Sunday morning, the last of my things had been packed, and we were ready to leave. The drive would take about four hours.

As we began the journey to Poughkeepsie, I turned and looked back at Arnant, but it was a different place. It would forever remind me of the summer I had escaped it to spend my days and nights as a Southwest Philly burnout drinking Bud on the corner of Paschall and Bonnaffon, playing arcade games at Titans, listening to heavy metal, racing cars and gang fighting on Holstein Avenue, dancing at the MacDade House and the R and L, exhilarating drives down Lindbergh Boulevard, and making out with Bobby. And, above all, a wrong turn that led me on the right path to a good and faithful friend named Lorraine.

As Daddy steered the van up I-95, he and Mummy talked to me at length about my week-long orientation, my course of study at Vassar, and even my path after graduation. I hardly spoke when I should have been gabbing excitedly. Noticing my sullenness, they left me alone. As they conversed between themselves, I smiled in wry amusement as the realization hit that the identity switch had been bookended by drives along I-95: this one, and the one that had forced me to execute an ill-planned detour that took me on a fateful trip into Southwest Philly.

When they weren't looking, I reached into my handbag, opened my wallet, located a small, secret compartment, and withdrew a piece of paper. It was the handbill that Bobby had been given at the MacDade

House that advertised the battle of the bands. I unfolded it, gazed at it, closed my eyes, and transported myself to those days.

I still have this handbill. The graphic is faded and barely legible, the creases separated and held together with tape, the paper yellowed and dog-eared. The damage has been inflicted on it from innumerable repetitions of extracting it from its hiding place, unfolding it, examining it, refolding it, and returning it to its hiding place. It has been transferred between an untold number of wallets over the years.

The handbill is the only tangible proof that my escapade during the summer of 1983 happened and wasn't some fantastic dream.

Lost in a reverie of Southwest Philly, heavy-metal music, arcade machines, and Delco dance halls, I watched I-95 slide by as I was carried off to the next chapter of my life. A chapter would probably never include Lorraine and would be haunted by memories of her and the summer she and I stepped away from our dull lives. Were we very brave or very stupid to pull off the identity switch? Even today, I still don't know.

PART FOUR

October 1983

to June 1988

Chapter Thirty

Lorraine

Time went by. I wanted to get in touch with Daven but was afraid to. It looked as if her parents made good on their threat to trace all her calls and check her mail because she never called me or wrote to me. I applied to Katharine Gibbs but never went there, much to Mom's great disappointment. In October of that year, I got a job doing data entry at an office in town. It wasn't the greatest job, but I survived on it. Eventually, I saved up enough money to rent an apartment at a duplex at 62nd and Reedland, about a mile from my neighborhood on Bonnaffon Street.

After that summer, I saw Bobby a few times around the neighborhood. Obviously, he didn't talk to me anymore. I told people we broke up for reasons I didn't want to talk about. He moved to Delco two years later, and I never saw or heard from him again.

Paulie and Deirdre had a daughter in February of 1984. They named her Sandra Joyce after Mom and Grandmom. They got married right after she was born, and I was the maid of honor. Paulie did go on to get his GED, and he was eventually promoted to manager of his store.

Joe DiGiacomo got busted for possession a few months later, during the summer of 1984. Turns out he was using Titans as a headquarters for his drug-dealing operation, and the sinister office guy Daven told me about was his enforcer. He got busted, too. Titans was closed and then reopened with a new owner under the name Video Warriors a few months later. But my days of playing arcade games were over, and I never went in there. Besides, there were too many painful reminders of Daven there. Video Warriors ended up closing in 1987. Today, it's a Dominican hair salon.

Grandmom's health kept getting worse. The COPD finally got the best of her, and we lost her in April of 1988.

I thought about Daven a lot and wondered how she was doing. Every so often, I would take the rose from the corsage Stuart gave me for the Stonehurst ball and cry, thinking about that magical summer of my life when I was able to escape Southwest Philly in more ways than one. The rose was the only proof I had that the identity switch ever happened. I still have that rose today. I keep it pressed between the pages of Grandmom's missalette, which I got after she died.

I thought about Daven and her family and friends and prayed for them every night and thanked God for giving me such a wonderful best friend, even if we couldn't talk to each other anymore.

As time passed, and the memories got blurry, I began to wonder if Daven and that summer ever happened at all. Sometimes, I thought it was a weird dream because it sure felt like it. Had a burnout like me really gone to a fancy ball in a Cinderella gown and danced with a guy who looked like a handsome prince? And had a debutante like Daven really drunk Bud on the corner of Paschall and Bonnaffon and bopped around to heavy metal at the MacDade House? It all seemed so unreal. Maybe it was best that I considered it all a dream in order to escape the heartbreak of never seeing Daven again.

v

One day, in June of 1988, exactly five years after me and Daven pulled off our identity switch, I was coming off the 36 trolley on my way home from work and saw something that stopped me dead in my tracks: a white 1988 BMW 320i, the kind of car you never see in Southwest Philly. It was parked right in front of my apartment building. The lady behind the wheel smiled at me, with a smile just like mine.

Author's Note

During my teenage years in the 1980s, my friends and I liked to amuse ourselves by finding doppelgangers for each other among celebrities. One friend bore a striking similarity to Mark Hamill of *Star Wars*, another to Elizabeth Taylor in her younger years. This silly game entertained us for hours. When I thought back to it, I wondered what would happen if two doppelgangers from opposite ends of the social spectrum came across each other and switched identities. Moreover, could I cull out of it a book set in my sweet spot: 1980s Southwest Philadelphia? Thus, the plot for my next book presented itself.

The cross-class relationship between Lorraine Kowalski and Daven Barrett was indeed unusual in the 1980s. Class differences were sharply defined during this era, and their boundaries were strictly enforced. So much so that cross-class relationships became an alluring and popular movie theme. The plots of several 1980s movies, i.e. *Valley Girl*; *Baby, It's You*; *Breathless*; *Pretty in Pink*; *Beaches*; *Dirty Dancing*; *Two Moon Junction*; and others, revolve around them and attest to their universal intrigue.

Lorraine and Daven are two examples of the major class types of the 1980s. Lorraine is a burnout. Such teenagers usually hailed from poor or working-class areas; engaged in alcohol, tobacco, and drug use; committed crimes; and either finished high school with poor grades or dropped out altogether. They were a largely invisible and overlooked demographic.

Their struggle was not regarded seriously.

Daven is a highly-privileged WASP who hails from a wealthy, socially-prominent family. Opportunity and privilege are her birthright. This places her at the top of the social ladder, unlike Lorraine, who is trapped at its bottom.

Each girl faces hardships imposed upon her by her social class. The struggles are obvious for Lorraine: unrelenting poverty, limited career opportunities, victimization by crime, and the struggle of single motherhood. But Daven faces struggles, too: she may be wealthy and privileged, but she has no control over her life. Others move her like a pawn on a chessboard and make her decisions for her.

In my first book, *The World I Know: The Diary of a Southwest Philly Girl*, characters from the Southwest Philadelphia 1980s burnout subculture are featured prominently in the story. The more I wrote about them, the more they intrigued me. I resolved that in my next book, one of the main characters would be a burnout. Thus, Lorraine Kowalski was born. Her high-society doppelganger, Daven Barrett, rushed into the world right behind her.

I was required to do quite a bit of research on Daven's wealthy WASP background, as it was a world largely unknown to me. During that research, I learned a great deal about it, and I learned right alongside Lorraine!

I hope I have presented, as realistically as possible, the worlds from which these girls hail and those worlds' particular cultures and customs. I hope you have enjoyed your trip back to the 1980s!

Celeste Harmer

Acknowledgments

I want to thank many people for their help in the birth of my second Southwest Philadelphia book. My good friend Brian Davey was again a dependable source of information and memories about Southwest Philly. Thank you, Brian!

My fan base has bolstered me, and I sincerely thank all of you for your inspiration.

I also want to give thanks not to a person but to a place: Southwest Philly, for giving me the beautiful memories it has and for playing a pivotal role in my upbringing, both of which have contributed to the books I have written.

Most of all, I would like to thank my husband, Ed, who encouraged and supported me as he read and reread the manuscript before it went to print. Thank you, my love, for putting up with Lorraine, Daven, and me!

Don't miss out!

Visit the website below and you can sign up to receive emails whenever Celeste Harmer publishes a new book. There's no charge and no obligation.

https://books2read.com/r/B-A-MXAKB-XKTDF

BOOKS 2 READ

Connecting independent readers to independent writers.

About the Author

Celeste Harmer is a native of Southwest Philadelphia and grew up in the nearby suburban town of Sharon Hill. She holds a Bachelor of Arts Degree in art history, Summa Cum Laude, from Rosemont College. She is the recipient of numerous academic awards and distinctions, chief among them selection for the All-Pennsylvania Academic Team, election to the post of president of the Alpha Tau Epsilon chapter of Phi Theta Kappa at Delaware County Community College, and membership in both the Alpha Omicron chapter of Delta Epsilon Sigma and the Gertrude Kistler Honor Society of Rosemont College.

Celeste's hobbies are art, physical fitness, and travel. She has both lived and traveled abroad, with her wanderings taking her to the Caribbean, Canada, Spain, and France, as well to much of the United States. She lives in the U.S. Virgin Islands with her husband Edward and their many cats.

Milton Keynes UK
Ingram Content Group UK Ltd.
UKHW020015061124
450708UK00001B/172